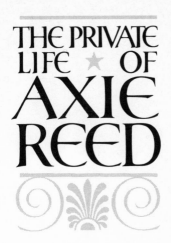

THE PRIVATE LIFE OF AXIE REED

JOHN KNOWLES

THE PRIVATE LIFE ★ OF AXIE REED

A William Abrahams Book

E. P. DUTTON / NEW YORK

ONE

1

This is the story of my cousin, the actress Alexandra Reed, as I remember it myself, and as I have been able to reconstruct it from the recollections of others.

My cousin Alexandra—Axie—always sensed that her life was worth recording—"there's a book in it, maybe a cautionary tale," she said on one occasion. She knew that she herself would not write it—"I couldn't sit still for it, too nervous, too flighty, no talent, something. *You* do it."

I never dreamed that I would, but then I never dreamed—no one did—of what would happen at the Parrish Art Museum Ball in Southampton, Long Island, in the summer of 1981.

2

Axie Reed always awoke early. As a little girl in Brooklyn Heights, in the dark old townhouse on the bluff overlooking the East River, she had had to get up very early for school, and during the summers, here in this house on Long Island, nothing could have kept her in bed once the sun was up—and the surf, as often as not, was up too—and perhaps Spyro would come by on his bike for an early tennis game or, a couple of years further on, in his pride and joy, a small Alfa-Romeo, wanting her to go sailing.

Early rising had of course been the rule at Purcell Academy in Massachusetts, and although at Sarah Lawrence it had been possible to sleep in occasionally, she had not wanted to. Alight with ambition, she was off at every opportunity to Manhattan, *to try out for plays*: how freighted with hope and aspiration and fear that phrase had once been for her, second only in importance and balefulness to *making the rounds.* At last both phrases and relentless habits had culminated in *getting a part,* and then another one, and then a *favorable mention by Brooks Atkinson,* and then *HOLLYWOOD.*

There, her ingrained habit of early rising had come into its own: all working Hollywood got up well before the crack of dawn and arrived, most of them, like zombies at makeup, surreptitiously popping pills and taking shots of God knew what to turn them into human beings before the cameras began to roll. Axie was almost alone in her freshness and cheerfulness and general sense of well-being at the earliest hour: she made jokes during makeup, while all around her reigned postsleep depression, hangover despair and predawn hopelessness. Many people said to her face that they hated her for it, but she knew better; while she was not exactly a little ray of morning sunshine in their estimation, they nevertheless could not fail to admire a metabolism so signally adapted to the weird, unnatural world of moviemaking. It had, however, been virtually the only thing about Hollywood which did come naturally to her.

This morning, through the cracks in the long draperies shutting it out, floods of August sunshine waited to be let into the room. Reaching out from her high four-poster bed, she pulled the old-fashioned cord and heard the archaic bell, faintly sounding in the kitchen in the back wing below. How opulent and old-fashioned it was. Her grandparents had put in bells and pulls to summon the staff of seven or so; she had Edna, and it seemed always had had Edna, and, God willing, always would have Edna, and so could go on living in a fragile, staff-of-one illusion of the manner this house had been designed to accommodate.

Axie settled back among her pillows, stretched her long, slender, catlike body contentedly, and thought: How wonderful to be able to be lazy. She knew that she alternated between laziness and almost compulsive, tireless work when it was necessary, and now, today, it was not necessary. She did not even have to be a hostess yet, sure that her two houseguests would not stir for an hour or two at least.

The sunshine was so obviously glorious behind those blocking draperies that she could not wait for Edna, bringing breakfast, to open them. Swinging her legs over the side of the high bed she swiftly stood up—and then felt an odd little sensation at the base of her skull, a kind of temporary numbness, and a strange momentary stab of dizziness too. She reached back and steadied herself with a hand on the bedpost, felt better—what had that been, too much wine at dinner last night?—and crossing to the two east windows, whipped back the draperies. Behind the filmy white curtains thus exposed, the freshest of morning sunrays poured down across the Atlantic Ocean, across Flying Point Beach, across Mecox Bay into her own treasured lifelong private place, Mill Creek Cove at Water Mill, Town of Southampton, and into this hospitable old mansion, Portals.

3

Edna, followed by Axie's dog Bruno, came in with the tray of her inevitable breakfast: a large glass of freshly squeezed orange juice; a bowl of hot oatmeal, winter and summer; one poached egg on white toast; two strips of thick-cut bacon; three cups of coffee. She ate a solid lunch every day too, and a substantial dinner. Axie exercised when she felt like it, never dieted, and never gained an ounce. Perhaps that had been the one other natural endowment she had possessed for being a movie star.

Edna was called "Mrs. Danvers" behind her back by Spyro, and in fact by all the Talouris family; the Talourises loved to mock people, and so did all Greeks, apparently. Edna did resemble that character in the novel and film *Rebecca* in two ways: She looked like her, with her very upright posture, black hair parted in the middle and pulled back into a prim bun; with her long-sleeved gray dress with white cuffs, and her rather severe, bony, handsome face. There was about her in general a certain forbidding aspect. The second point of resemblance between Edna and Mrs. Danvers was in her utter devotion to her mistress. Edna would, as a matter of course and without question, instantly lay down her life for Alexandra Reed if necessary. Axie knew that, and Edna knew that Axie knew it.

But here all resemblance stopped. Instead of the chill, almost demonic character of Mrs. Danvers, Edna was, despite her exterior, a gentle, considerate creature, tentative, sensitive, incapable of hurting a fly.

That is, unless in defense of Axie. There had been that film made in France, at the Victorine Studio in Nice, when at the height of a furious quarrel the director, beside himself, had slapped Axie. Edna had instantly sprung at him and wildly clawed his face, drawing blood.

That had been the last quarrel on the set. The picture was completed without further incident and became one of Axie's greatest hits.

Bruno, the German shepherd, all black and silver and taut intelligence, sprang at a bound onto the bottom of the bed, calculatedly far enough away not to spill the breakfast tray. Bruno was as close to perfect as a dog could be, but even Bruno, Axie surmised, was not quite as totally devoted to her as was Edna.

"Is it as beautiful a day as it looks from here?" Axie asked between mouthfuls.

"It is. More beautiful."

Hearing this, Axie hurried through the rest of her breakfast, slipped her feet into mules, threw a long white terry-cloth robe around her, and, trailed with a purposeful tread by Bruno, strode out of her room, across the balustraded landing, and started down the wide staircase.

Again, suddenly, a momentary dizziness came over her at the sight of the stairs. She grabbed the banister, and the dizziness vanished as quickly as it had come. What *had* she had to drink last night? It couldn't have been all that much in her case because she never drank all that much.

Continuing, a shade more carefully, to the bottom of the stairs, she crossed the spacious front hall and stepped out the door, across the circle of graveled driveway and onto the wide lawn, which sloped gently to the cove, her cove.

Three swans glided thoughtfully along the water there, and beyond it the wide expanse of Mecox Bay gleamed with morning's dazzle in the fresh sunshine. In the distance stretched the sandbar beach, and beyond that, still a little obscured in the last of dawn's haze, the Atlantic Ocean.

One thing about Hollywood, Los Angeles; it had been, at least, on an ocean—the wrong ocean, an odorless, rather inert mass of water, but still and all, an ocean—and that had made it possible for her to spend five otherwise laborious and charmless years there. Had the American movie capital been in Kansas City she would have never had a film career at all.

Axie turned to look at the house, her house. It was, in her estimation, the most beautiful, ideal domestic dwelling in the United States. It was just plain perfect. And it came to her there on the lawn this August morning that this particular place was the only thing in her life that came remotely close to that word, *perfect*.

Her career as an actress? Good Lord, blunders and

flops and might-have-beens, with an occasional performance in a play or a movie that amounted to something,
said something, made a difference. Douglas, who had "discovered" her, had always maintained that she was too
"analytical," as he put it, to be a movie actress, and perhaps
that was why that career had so dissatisfied her.

And now, surely, the career was over. She would be
fifty years old next month, and there were not going to
be any more parts for her, not starring parts anyway, and
she would accept no other. It was over. And so was, it
seemed, her ambition for it. For someone who had been
devoured by an obsession to act since age twelve, this
recently recognized void in her psyche surprised her, almost stunned her. Where there had been an overwhelming
presence—to be an actress, a star!—there now seemed to
be a space, an emptiness, a vacuum.

Nature, she knew, abhorred such things, such vacan-
cies, and at the back of her mind, behind her thoughts,
something stirred: a possible new drive, new ambition,
something to fill perhaps this lately discovered vacuum.

Yes, she had been a star of stage and screen, and it
had in the long run disappointed her, though the studios
and the Broadway producers had by and large not been
disappointed. She was a "draw," she could pull them in
off the streets. And then her marriage hadn't worked out
either in the long run; she had no children. Despite its
glitter her life had all been, to her, secretly, a disappointment.

The one thing that had never disappointed her was
this place, this house and these five acres of lawn and
gardens and trees surrounding it, her home, Portals. She
turned to look at the long, gleaming, white clapboard
structure, its turn-of-the-century windows flanked com-

panionably by dark gray shutters, the deep porch with one-
story wooden Ionic pillars, the recessed little balcony above,
and the peaked attic level with its two long fan windows
like Oriental eyes. The only disappointment or heartbreak
these four walls which had sheltered her for a lifetime could
inflict on her would be to burn down. And if that catas-
trophe should God forbid happen, well then she would
pitch a tent, out here on the lawn, and still be able to lose
herself in the splendid, serene view, and still become im-
mersed in the odors, from the great spruces, the mown
grass, the flowers.

But as she strolled over the moist, clipped lawn in her
white robe, her tousled dark blond hair falling to her shoulders, a slender figure, the head instinctively carried high,
she reflected that few people would share her disappointment in herself, her life. Was she not the special, enviable
Alexandra Reed, sprung from old family and old money
and prestigious schools, and wife—well, ex-wife—of one
of the Golden Greek Talourises, age nearly fifty but looking thirty-five—on top, it would seem, as she had always
been in her own special way, of her own special world?

She continued her walk. What a glorious morning.
She must not brood; she had never been the brooding type.

4

This is that morning in the life of Axie Reed as I was later
able to reconstruct it, by talking at length about it with

Axie, and with Edna—Mrs. Purvis—and by recollecting it visually. For as Axie had made this strolling tour of her property in that morning's sunshine, I happened to have pulled back my own draperies and was looking across at Mecox Bay when Axie had come out across the porch and the gravel driveway, Bruno dashing ahead of her and then waiting for her to overtake him. She had looked particularly striking that morning, something tall and slender and almost regal in her stride and yet an isolation visible too, almost a poignancy, an aloneness, a lovely no-longer-young famous lady, alone on this brilliant morning on her few hereditary acres, with her faithful German shepherd, and perhaps, in the last analysis, not much else.

Yes, she had one other thing: her character, her personality, her force, not the imitation Axie Hollywood had manufactured but the real one, driving, special, utterly human Cousin Axie.

I got into a bathrobe and slippers and went out into the back hall, up to the balustraded landing, down the wide stairway, out onto the porch.

Edna materialized behind me, asking what I wanted for breakfast. I asked for coffee, juice, roll, to eat out here on the porch, close to this brilliant morning, to the lawn and the lapping water of the cove with its three gliding swans, close to romping Bruno, and close to my drifting, graceful, solitary cousin, a white figure now striding across the grass toward me.

"Is there anywhere in the world you would rather be than here?" she asked with a wide smile.

"Nowhere, absolutely nowhere." I knew my lines with Axie.

"Edna is bringing you some breakfast? Good. I wonder how long we'll have to wait before Miss Marsh deigns to join us. Journalists aren't famous for getting up early in the morning, are they?"

"That particular journalist you've got in your second-best guest room upstairs *is* famous for sensing a story. She can probably hear us murmuring together right now, in her sleep. I'd expect her down here fairly soon if I were you."

Nor was I wrong. By the time Axie had gotten to her room and changed into a white blouse and dark blue slacks, and I had changed to some slacks and a polo shirt and come back down to the porch, Pauline Marsh was ready for her leisurely-appearing, thought-out entrance. She came out onto the porch wearing a sunflower-yellow tennis dress and Jacqueline Onassis oversized sunglasses, asking if there was a morning paper around. We gave her that week's issue of the *Southampton Press*. "What in the world?" she murmured almost to herself after scanning it for a minute. " 'Bid to Ban Vehicles on Bay Beaches,' 'Solution to Garbage Crisis Could Be Costly'!" She gazed through her lenses in bewilderment, real or feigned, over the top of the paper at us. "This is news? Are they serious?"

"Darling, you're in the country," Axie interceded in her low-pitched, penetrating, effortless voice. "You know that. We don't have big sensational news here. You must know that, too."

Looking back over that morning I recollected these words of Axie's with special poignance, for she had when she said them momentarily forgotten that people were news, and in the month of August in the year of Our Lord 1981, this East End of Long Island had newsworthy people, famous people, world-renowned people tucked away in many mansions and cottages and sailboats and yachts. We even had one, herself, here.

"Did Edna bring you breakfast?" she asked.

"Oh no, no," murmured Pauline, "just coffee. I don't breakfast in the country. Or in the city, really. Or lunch. Just, you know, dinner." She was small, black-haired, athletic-looking, without an extra ounce on her body, whipcord. Languorous, as Douglas would have said, she wasn't.

Axie, prone on a yellow couch on this long East Porch, her final cup of morning coffee balanced on her slender stomach, turned to gaze for perhaps the thirty-thousandth time in her life at the long, serene, peaceful perspective before her. She took a deep, calm breath. "Sitting here," she said in her husky voice, "you would never know how many changes are going on around you, out here on the East End." She never referred to the area as the Hamptons, leaving that to the society and gossip pages. For her it was and always had been the East End, flat rich land of potato farmers, and of the sea, unpredictable preserve of fishermen.

Pauline Marsh, the Washington photojournalist, obviously thought that her rather pointed nose smelled the first waftings of a story. "Well, what *is* changing out here, exactly? I mean, some things are obvious, but you know the area in depth. What's the real . . ." *story* she almost said, but then her caginess intervened: catch them off guard, even if you're their houseguest, even if they have no idea they're being interviewed: "What's the real—underlying change?"

Axie sighed dramatically. The dramatic sound and gesture came naturally to her, whether she intended them or not, she could not help herself. "Well, I'm sure you've noticed all the new houses going up, like toadstools in the middle of our potato fields, and the *con-do-miniums* sprawling now around the villages, and the choked traffic on Montauk Highway. But that's not what you would call the underlying change. The underlying change is in the manners. The people out here, what are called the 'locals'— I hate that word, so condescending-sounding—they've been reserved people. They're New Englanders, of course, their ancestors are. Came here from Massachusetts and Connecticut around 1630 or so, put up their New England villages with the Green and the white-steepled Congregational Church, put up the stocks for the lady shrews and men drunkards to be locked into when they were especially naughty, then all the villagers came by and spat in their faces or something, better than shock treatment or group therapy any day if you ask me. And it more or less went on like that until about the time grandfather built this house, didn't it, Nick, around the turn of the century. People like us began to come here, in the summers. Southampton and then East Hampton got fashionable. But that was all right, we went away in September and everything continued as before, and there weren't really so many of us, and we didn't interfere so much, and we brought them *money,* didn't we, and they were *New Englanders,* Yankees, weren't they, canny, knew the value of a dollar, so they tolerated us, made money off us, and all was pretty much peace and harmony. But *now!*" A dramatic pause: the great eyes widened, her voice sank to its leonine growl: "Now too many people are coming, and throwing their weight around, and the place is turning into an annex of New York City, and New York City manners are coming right along with it. And that's shocked the people who've always lived here, and their guards are up, they're nervous and they're jumpy and they're . . . pissed off." Her chin sank

pseudorural, all ensconced in the tended and tempered greenness of summer's lawns and shrubbery and great soaring leaf-heavy trees; the wafting scents of nature, indigenous and imported, filled the lightly breezy air, which turned salty as Main Street terminated near the off-white, fine-sanded beach, where stylish swimmers and cavorting kids made sand castles in the sunshine.

This was the happy time, when the privileged people enjoyed their privileges, when well-maintained bodies sought their fulfillment in the surf and on the golf course and together, in bed. Someone would smash up in a car; there would be a terrible family row somewhere, violence maybe, a stabbing; a woman would nearly drown in the surf. But for the most part, it was all pleasure and health and fun and games, flirtation and fulfillment and forgetfulness, here among the huge trees and the spreading lawns and the endless-seeming corridor of sand disappearing into the diaphanous sunshine shimmer off toward Montauk.

The ball that evening, a dinner-dance in benefit of Southampton Hospital, was the climax of the social season for the social people in the social part of Southampton. Axie had never gone to it before, because she had avoided as much as she decently could the social people and the social season there. "I'm a worker," she liked to say, and to mean. "I've always been a professional. I haven't got time for all these fetes and festivities." This year, however, she had been persuaded to take a table for the ball. It was for a very worthy cause, after all. The image of health herself, she nevertheless knew abstractly that hospitals were very important to others. Since she'd had no children, hospitals had virtually never entered into her life. But she understood that they were important to others, and so she agreed to take this table at the ball. It would help her entertain her houseguests, moreover. When people came to Southampton in the summer, they expected to see beautiful people, parties, jewelry. So tonight she would show her two houseguests, these ill-matched and just-met guests, Nick Reed and Pauline Marsh, the pretty glitter embedded in a Southampton summer.

That evening at 7:30 P.M. precisely I stood in front of one of those large circular mirrors found in older houses like this, and looked at myself in dinner jacket and black tie. I was seven years younger than my cousin Axie, and I will have to say in fairly good shape. Perhaps it was in the genes: Axie remained remarkably lithe and youthful, and so apparently did I: square shoulders, five feet ten, 170 pounds, with lots of skiing and some mountain-climbing and endless biking and things like that built in. Those exertions, I think, were in the genes, too. The Reeds had originally been Vermont people, and they were hardy, hiking, snowshoeing, climbing people, outdoors people, farming people, dairy people. Axie's line had then gone into banking and come to New York and gotten kind of rich, mine into academia and gone to Amherst and Cambridge and gotten kind of scholarly.

I went out into the hall and started across the landing toward the stairs. Axie spied me—she rarely missed anything anywhere in her surroundings—as I passed, reflected in her mirror, and called, "Come in here and help me choose a bauble; keep me from looking garish."

She stood dressed and ready before her full-length gilt-framed mirror, only the selection of a jewel or two remaining.

The room was high-ceilinged, with its high four-poster bed, a Hepplewhite highboy, a frivolous white-satin-draped vanity table, Persian rug and filmy summer curtains beside the wide, long windows, with their spectacular view of the bay, and the tiny lights of the beach across it. There was a small curved-top fireplace with a family portrait above it, of a joint New England ancestor of ours, a parson. There was her writing table, and a floor-to-ceiling book-case.

This was in every sense Alexandra's room; she slept in it, studied scripts and answered mail in it, read in it, and, with the very few men she felt she had truly loved, I am sure made love in it.

She now held two diamond clips at the neckline of her shimmering light blue sheath. "Too much?"

"Mm . . ." I hedged: I had no judgment in her clothes, always liking the way she looked.

"No. Mother's diamond bracelet, then. Just that." She contemplated the result in the mirror, then, reluctantly, it seemed, added diamond drop earrings. She stepped back and looked critically at herself in the mirror.

The lighting in this room was the only thing done in it by a professional decorator. The rest had been entirely chosen and arranged by her, but she had not been a big movie star for nothing. For truly effective lighting you needed a professional. So here in the large corner bedroom there was subdued, flattering, soft lighting, and standing before her mirror she had to see that, frankly, she looked beautiful. There was a self-critical, pessimistic woman lurking within ebullient Axie Reed, but even this aspect of her personality seemed to acquiesce this evening in my estimation of her: a tall, slender, glamorously beautiful woman.

Slipping her hand under my arm she walked—swept— the evening was already turning into an occasion—out across the landing to the wide stairway. Standing waiting in the hall below was Pauline Marsh in green silk. "You're ready!" Axie called gaily down to her. "Good! We're off to the ball, and no one's wearing glass slippers."

6

Afterward, this ball was remembered for two things: the elegance and élan of the party itself, and then, the event that abruptly put a halt to it. It was held beneath a great white silken marquee, with silver and blue balloons and streamers, vivid flower arrangements on each table, a raised dance floor and a ten-piece band. Waiters swiftly finished preparing for the three hundred guests, champagne began to flow, glittering dresses and gleaming hair and flashing jewels competed against and were complemented by the elegantly festive setting itself.

Axie's seven dinner guests would have fun, she would see to that. Axie was a born crowd-pleaser, which was of course a prime reason for her success both in the theater and in the movies.

Her guests, in addition to the two of us from Portals, were an art museum director from Massachusetts and his wife, an Austrian countess from Newport, Rhode Island, an American automobile heir who seemed to have barely heard of a place called Detroit, and a Wall Street polo player.

As we were making our way to this table through a

clutter of party-goers, the women looking by and large pretty or at least striking-looking or else unarguably rich, the men pulled-together-looking, Axie confided in my ear, "They wanted me to be 'social' tonight so our table is full of social people. And I wanted to impress that journalist woman from Washington."

"Why did you invite her for the weekend, anyway?"

"She more or less invited herself. And you don't trifle with Pauline Marsh. She can make you look pretty ridiculous in print if she wants to."

So we joined our table and the courses of the dinner were whisked on and off, the food quite good; red wine, white wine, and champagne kept falling and then rising again in our glasses, the dance tunes bounced and swung around us, and as couples began to mount the steps to the dance floor it was clear that this was the climax of another successful Southampton summer season.

From an adjacent table Keith Miller strolled across and asked Axie Reed to dance. Keith was one of the handful of movie people who spent their summers here, and he and his fragile wife had fitted right in, as people said. Tall, sandy-haired, spectacled, he looked more like an in-demand college professor than a successful Hollywood producer-director. "Come on, Axie, you look too great to just sit there," he said, bending down close to her ear as the band played a swingy version of Cole Porter's "Get Out of Town." "I want to show you off up there on the dance floor." She was looking up at him hesitatingly.

"Oh Keith—I—my guests—"

"Forget about your guests. They're in your cousin's capable hands there." He frowned down at her slightly; he knew her, she disliked to displease. "Come on."

She rose, they mounted the steps to the raised dance floor, and he, taller than she and almost as lithe, began to sail with her gracefully around the only moderately crowded floor.

A number of people paused to admire the glittering, slender figure of the unique Alexandra Reed, the famous mane of dark blond hair falling to her shoulders, the few diamonds sparkling here and there—this member of a fine old Southampton and Brooklyn Heights family but since become a *movie* star, fancy that combination, quite special, you see, but we all admire her and she's never "gone Hollywood" as they say or used to say, never lost her natural charm nor her innate sense of background, yes we're all so fond of Axie—the diners noticed her as she was becoming caught up in this easy graceful dance and in what her partner was saying: "Axie, you still just look too good to have given up acting, the movies. What is this rumor about your retirement! You can't retire."

"They don't write my kind of movie any more."

"It's a waste," said Keith.

"It's *not* a waste! I plan to be very active in—in social work—you know, committees—social work—help *others* for a change. Being an actress—a *star,*" she added, a little smile and a wide stare mocking the concept, "is so bloody selfish."

"Listen to your own voice. It's so expressive, and it's got feminine authority, yet it's vulnerable, breakable, I don't know. If you've heard the growl of that bitch I had to direct in my last picture."

"I heard," she commented laconically.

"Then you know how badly we need you. These little *girls* they find for us in, I don't know, Nogales!" He groaned in her ear.

"That bad."

"Worse. Come back to Hollywood."

"Oh, please. You know my movie career is finished. All they'd want me for now is somebody's mother, or else an axe-murderess."

"That's changing. Listen, there's a great part for you in—"

"Darling," she said cajolingly, "not tonight, I beg you. Mercy, have mercy. Come tomorrow for a swim in our cove. Then—" she drew a sudden breath.

"What happened? I step on your foot? I'm really sorry."

"No, I just felt a . . . it's nothing."

"You want to sit down?"

"No. It's all right. Oh I love this tune."

The band had modulated into "You Do Something to Me."

So Keith swept her on around the floor and they had just reached the front of the platform, just above and next to the table where Axie's guests were, where we were all looking up smilingly at the handsome couple. Then Axie seemed to catch the heel of her right slipper on something, although there was nothing to catch it on, she turned inside his arms, slipped out of them, another half-turn and, her eyes glassy, fell turning from the dance floor onto the grass next to the table below. As we all sat aghast, for an instant unable to react, Pauline Marsh in one motion slid her hand into her oversized bag, pulled out her tiny flash camera and, poised above Axie, whose head, framed in her dark gold hair, lay face up, snapped a news photograph.

TWO

7

That was how the people who had been closest to Axie all of her life, and the public in general, learned of her collapse: a horrific news photo of her expressive face, framed by an aureole of her hair, stricken, on the grass, eyes like slits, shot mercilessly from above.

It was an August Sunday morning, one of the slowest, dullest days of the year for newspapers. Axie had been intermittently famous for almost thirty years: this news photo, blown up to two-column or three-column or four-column size, ran all over the country and in various parts of the rest of the world.

Lambros Talouris, immaculate in white silk suit, having his Turkish coffee in his favorite café around the corner from the Grande Bretagne Hotel in Athens, found it staring out at him from the English-language newspaper. He sat motionless, as stricken seemingly as she had been at the moment of attack, and then he very slowly and fiercely crumpled the newspaper up in his fist. To the passing waiter, he said harshly out of the side of his mouth: "Ouzo!"

Spyro Talouris had spent the night in a marina in Sag Harbor, a few miles from Southampton on Peconic Bay, aboard his forty-one-foot sloop, the *Electra*. He had spoken by telephone to Axie the previous afternoon and upon being told by her that she was taking a fashionable group of friends to the fashionable ball he had remarked drily, "You've sold out at last, sweetheart, haven't you?" to which Axie, catching his mood, had replied swiftly, "Just because they won't let you Greeks in . . ." It had been a typically lighthearted and mock-insulting conversation between them, the sort they had been exchanging virtually since they had learned to talk.

Spyro had been married for twenty years to Janie, a devoted wife, and he was the father of four children. While fulfilling his role as husband and father intensely, he yet somehow maintained a private and even bachelor streak in his life. Janie was accommodating. Today neither she nor any of the children was with him.

This Sunday morning, in white bell-bottom sailing pants and a loose blue shirt, Spyro, feeling good, walked briskly up Sag Harbor's Main Street in search of a morning newspaper. A few flags and pennants snapped in the breeze, and the wide street with low storefronts on both sides was busy with strollers and sailors and children and dogs. Spyro reached a stationery store, turned in, and went up to the piles of the Sunday *New York Times* and *Newsday*. Reaching them, he started to pick both of them up when he experienced a sort of faint pricking in his peripheral vision. Spyro turned, looked down at the top copy of the *New York Daily News* next to them, and beheld the almost full-page photo of Axie's face, seemingly lying stricken there on the floor of the store. Jerkily, he snatched up the paper and began glaring at it, then leafing confusedly through the pages in a dazed search for the text of the story, roaming out of the store, forgetting the other newspapers, forgetting to pay.

At the ball itself, it had not been immediately apparent to most people what had happened. Axie had left the dance floor; a flash bulb had gone off; nothing remarkable in that. But then, like rings of water spreading outward from some fallen object, the consternation spread slowly, then with speed. The band had reached

> Let me live 'neath your spell,
> Do do that voodoo that you do so well . . .

when the leader, at last sensing an emergency, stopped them. A hanging, strange silence spread beneath the glittering tent, and then out-of-control voices began to ring out.

"Where is—I know I saw—Dr. Smithers over at that table!" "Don't crowd around! Should we lift her?" "Don't touch her!" I heard myself yelling as I knelt beside her. Someone cried, "Her neck may be broken!" Other voices: "Oh my *God*! It's Axie!" "Call an ambulance!" "Call a doctor!" "Call the police!"

Pauline Marsh was leaning over behind me. "Get out

of here," I heard myself snarl at her, "with that camera."

Then Dr. Smithers was beside me, and I pulled back a little as his hands began carefully, gently to touch her here and there.

A siren could be heard approaching, and in a couple of minutes more the paramedic team had arrived and taken charge.

Axie herself was passing into a painful world of confused dreams and muffled, hysterical voices. There was a weird paralysis at the base of her head, next to her spine. She now suddenly felt far, far too fatigued to attempt to move. Perhaps she would never move again, never have to; she would be carried everywhere like Cleopatra, either Claudette Colbert's or Elizabeth Taylor's, take your pick, on a litter. Oh those hysterical, distant, then close, voices! Would they never never stop!

But then there was a sudden silence, a smoothness, she was rolling smoothly in some vehicle, and the atmosphere was suddenly soothing, after all that racket. There was to be sure a siren to be heard close at hand, but that was somehow soothing too.

A short time later she seemed to be in a tent, and that was appropriate for Cleopatra also. She recollected in her cotton-wool-wrapped mind, her slowed mind, the visit to Egypt with Lambros, the trip up the Nile by riverboat; she could see in her mind's eye the reddish-brown banks of the river again, and the low, cubist, ironically modern-looking houses, hovels out of the bronze age, and the tiny children in tattered dresses calling out to them, calling something . . . something, running along the bank, trying to keep up with the boat, and calling . . . calling . . .

8

I had been sitting for four hours in a waiting room at Southampton Hospital. Pauline Marsh, whom I now frankly and openly hated—my anger at whatever had injured Axie fastening swiftly if irrationally on this woman who had found in this disaster a photo opportunity—Pauline Marsh was nothing if not dogged, and she sat with me, although a prudent two chairs away. "Why don't you go back to the house?" I said flatly from time to time, but she continued to sit there. A half hour before, I had persuaded Keith Miller and the others to leave. Pauline only replied once: "You shouldn't be alone," and I suppose she was right. But why did my solitude have to be relieved by her?

She had not been with me in the waiting room the entire time, having disappeared when the ball broke up and reappeared near but not at my side some time later.

A fatigued-looking orderly came out and said, "There's no news yet. You can't see her."

I had taken off my black tie—what an absurd item of male clothing it looked as I pulled it off, a thin strip of black silk, or satin, or whatever it was made of. Who invented it? Beau Brummel? I was beginning to look unshaven, as though that mattered, and, glancing over my shoulder at Pauline Marsh, I saw that she had a tired and rumpled look too. "Go home . . . go back to Portals," I said to her again flatly. She looked at me.

I got up, found a telephone, and called a taxi. When the driver came into the waiting room, Pauline stood up, murmuring, "Gosh I'm so sorry; call me if—"

I nodded abstractedly, staring at the floor, and she left.

The room had the kind of flat, unblinking illumination seemingly designed to induce depression in anyone sitting in it, especially anyone awaiting news of a stricken "loved one"—Axie had now fallen into that sentimental category in my life, a "loved one," like some frail elderly aunt. I was the only person waiting there. There were no magazines; I did not smoke.

After a while I began to pace. I had always thought that nervous, suspense-filled people only paced in the movies; Axie had done quite a pacing scene in *Just Before Dawn*. Perhaps as I strode back and forth in this sterile room, hands locked at the base of my spine, I had become life imitating art, although come to think of it *Just Before Dawn* had not been a work of art: it had been a potboiler.

Then a rather compact man in white with grayish hair came out and said, "Are you Miss Reed's relative? I'm Dr. LaBrianca. Let's sit down. No, no, don't jump to any conclusions. She isn't—" We sat down. "She is your cousin, is that correct? Our switchboard here has been flooded with calls. I'm not much of a moviegoer myself, haven't the time. But I see here tonight that your cousin is quite famous, and the newspapers and TV people and many many friends are frankly swamping our switchboard." He looked at me and I looked at him. "Oh, I am—I'm sorry. Yes, her condition. She's holding her own, yes, well she's critical, she's, well, very critical, and there is . . . should Miss Reed sink into deep coma, there is a real possibility that we might not be able to bring her out of it. That would be, well, that could be fatal. But. She has not sunk into a coma *yet,* and with each passing hour, if she fights . . ." He looked at me. "She is fifty, our records show? Well, if she puts up a fight, it is that, if it is to be anything, which will pull her through. We are doing everything possible, and now we will simply have to wait and see."

Finally I said to him in a slow and even voice, "What in hell happened to her? One moment she's beautiful, dancing, the next—"

"We will test for the reason for the collapse eventually. Had she been having dizzy attacks, do you know?"

"I don't know."

"Well, it might have been many things. But you see, beyond that, she was injured, very seriously injured in the fall."

I stared at him. "There was a steel brace," he went on matter-of-factly, "sticking out from under that platform, that temporary platform, supporting it. It is pyramid-shaped, almost pointed. Falling from that height at just the wrong angle Miss Reed fell against it with her right rib cage. Several of her ribs are broken. That in itself would not be very serious, but the shattered ribs ripped open her right lung, and there is serious, very serious internal bleeding, and we have not . . . yet . . . been able to stop it. The bleeding is continuing, and it is *that* which is the danger. Of course we are giving her transfusions, large quantities of blood. But this is all a severe shock, a very severe shock to the system of a fifty-year-old woman. If she does not fight hard, we, well then . . . I would not be able to hold out much hope for her . . . chances. As it is. Well. We will only be able to wait and see. We are doing everything possible."

We sat there for a period. "There is something you can do."

I focused on his face.

"Go home," he said quietly. "Then our switchboard here, our overworked ladies, can transfer the calls there, and you can take that load off the hospital. You will be up the rest of the night, you will be up until you take your telephone off the hook. But if you are there answering even for an hour or two, it will help."

I stood up; I shook his hand.

Then I went out into the parking lot, got into my Pontiac, and started toward Portals along the side road not far from the beach. I was of course the only car driving along it; indeed mine seemed to be the only car in motion on Long Island. I glanced down the flat sweep of potato fields toward the dunes and the ocean; dawn had not yet begun to break, but it was a starry August night and a ghostly wraithlike version of the East End could be discerned: rows of potato plants disappearing toward the hump of dunes; the odd tiny light here and there at the beach, with just a hint, a dream of surf beyond. Axie had loved these nights.

9

Just after I left for home, Axie was wheeled from the emergency room to the intensive care unit. Dr. LaBrianca had already performed several procedures in his attempt to save her life. Immediately after the first swift examination, when the broken ribs and the internal bleeding had been established, he cut open with a scalpel the flesh under her right arm; there was already a crease there, a crease caused by aging, and Dr. LaBrianca cut for approximately one inch along that crease: any disfigurement would be negligible. A tube was slipped into this incision and extended down into the cavity around the ripped right lung, into the blood which had escaped there, and the draining out of that blood began.

Into Axie's left arm another tube began replacing the blood; her blood pumping out on one side, the blood of other people pumping in on the other. But the internal bleeding continued. Then the platelet count in her blood, an element necessary in clotting, began to drop, seemingly unstoppably. Axie began to fade, to fade toward deep shock. Then her right lung collapsed.

She continued to drift in a boat, sometimes up the Nile toward Aswan, but this riverboat was metamorphosed after a while into the Talouris yacht, the *Pacificus,* very long, very white, with powerful diesel engines and staterooms and saloons and even a small swimming pool and a seaplane and a motor launch . . . the *Pacificus* was slicing through the green-blue Aegean like an ivory-white knife, knifing through the lightly tossing sea in the glitter of morning's sunlight—just like the sunlight this morning—was it this morning?—when she had strolled on the lawn . . . strolled with Bruno in front of Portals? Was she on Long Island? Had Nick Reed been an overnight guest?

I am in a hospital, she gradually assembled her senses enough to realize. I was at a party, that ball at the art museum. Then I—something happened—no idea what—but I have been injured. I have been very seriously injured.

I am in a hospital. When I try to look up I seem to be in a tent, but I know now that I am not in a tent. I have been very seriously injured somehow—maybe God has struck me with a bolt of lightning for my sins.

Things are broken in me. I cannot move.

Things are broken, interior parts of my body. I don't know what they are—blood vessels, bones, I can't tell—but the breakage, I can tell that, can feel that. Much has been broken. Too much, maybe too much.

I don't believe, she confided to herself in a cosmically calm voice, a calm voice speaking almost into eternity, I don't believe I can come back from this. I'm dying, I think.

I am so tired, so very very endlessly tired. And I can't move, not a muscle.

But then I don't want to move. I am sinking—the boat, the riverboat or else the *Pacificus* is sinking, slowly, oh really slowly, but also unstoppably, it is sinking beneath me, and I am broken, many things are broken in me, and I can't move, and I am utterly crushed by exhaustion, and I believe that this is nearing the end of my life, it is unstoppable, and if this is to be the end then . . . well . . .

But I am not dying, if I am dying, before I have lived. Because I have lived. Yes, thank God, I am not dying before I have lived.

Twenty years ago, fifteen even, I would be going mad now, out of rage at not having really lived.

But now I am slowly and unstoppably sinking and that is all right, that is all right if it has to be, because with all the disappointments, with all the only partial quality of my life—it was only partial, only part of what I dreamed of, of what might have been—still I know that I drew much . . . many things out of life; I did not let it go by me untasted, unseized.

Too much is broken, and I am sinking toward the end, but this is not happening before I have lived.

10

I turned my car into Cobb Road in Water Mill. What had that doctor been saying? What he had been saying was: Axie might die; Axie probably would die.

It was grotesque, before it was shocking or saddening, it was simply grotesque. This radiant cousin of mine, this lifelong womanly athlete, who never missed a performance in any play, never a day's work in any film, who could dance all night and three hours later be on the tennis court, generally winning—that Alexandra Reed was sinking toward death had not yet even become a shocking or saddening thought for me, it was quite simply grotesque, as though Mecox Bay, off there on my right, were filling up with sand and ceasing to be water: ridiculous, grotesque.

I came to the high wooden gateposts of Portals, and turned into the long, straight gravel driveway, the great overhanging trees leading up to the high, brown-shingled water tower; I curved around to the right of that and came up to the house, to the circle of driveway in front of the East Porch.

What were those lights doing on in the living room? Axie was in the hospital; Edna would be asleep in serene ignorance. It was not fitting to have the lights on: the house should be darkened, suspended and waiting.

And then I remembered Pauline Marsh. Oh no.

I was going to have to confront the bitch-photographer, here in Axie's house, just the two of us in the pre-dawn. Drawing a deep, sighing breath, I got out of the car and walked across the porch, through the front doorway, across the high, spacious entrance hall, and, turning right, came into the high, square, many-windowed living room. Pauline was curled up, childlike, in a corner of the long white couch, legs tucked under her, reading glasses, beguilingly I suppose she thought, on her nose, perusing a book.

She looked up, on cue, as I came in. Lucky for you, you never tried for a career in acting, I remarked to myself.

Pauline sprang up, putting down the book, snatching off the glasses. How many times did you rehearse this, I wondered. "How is she?" she breathed. "She's going to be all right, isn't she?"

I stood in front of her. "We don't know, they don't know yet," I said expressionlessly.

"What on earth was it?"

"They don't know yet. But what we didn't realize—I didn't realize at the party—is that she didn't just collapse, faint, or whatever happened. She also—" I went on more grimly— "was injured in the fall. Very—seriously—injured."

"Oh no. What is—"

Abruptly I cut in: "What did you do with that picture?"

She frowned at me as though to dissimulate and ask, "What picture?" but one glance at my face made her instantly abandon that tactic. "The picture is—well it's—you know—gone."

"Gone. Gone where?"

"Gone. You know. Filed."

"Does that mean it can be printed?"

"Well—yes." And I'm not apologizing for that, her demeanor added.

Suddenly I realized how tired I was. What difference, after all, did the photograph really make? It would not change Axie's desperate condition, whether it was printed or not. If it was printed, it would shock a lot of people, but Axie was, as the lawyers said, a public figure, and her rights to privacy were therefore compromised legally. When she chose that career, she threw away many of her rights to privacy. What's more, she had invited this woman into her house as a guest.

I slowly made my way across the room and dropped into a deep armchair near the grand piano.

"You look really bushed," Pauline Marsh remarked.

I took a slow breath. "The telephone is going to start ringing," I then said. "They're transferring calls from the hospital. They sent me here to answer them."

"So," she reflected aloud, "nobody's there at the hospital sort of, you know, standing by." I looked at her with a flicker of curiosity. "I could go and wait there, just in case of anything." I then discerned a sliver of humanity shining through the harsh glare of her personality. A nice, bright little girl lay submerged somewhere within this tough young baggage. And from lack of exposure that little girl would one of these days expire, too, I supposed.

Too? *Too?* What did I mean by *too*!

Axie must fight, she had to fight, that was her hope, her chance. And she would, of course she would.

The telephone rang. The living room telephone was beside my chair, and I picked it up rather slowly, reluctantly, but—this was now my job, the one thing I could contribute—with a resigned sense of duty.

It was the Associated Press. From then until dawn and well after dawn, the telephone rang every few minutes, and in my recollection, the conversations merged into a continuum of reportorial questions, with an occasional friend or co-worker of Axie's being able to break into the chain of calls. The reporters' questions involved exactly what had happened at the ball, and what I knew about her physical condition. But then the questions began to modulate, it seemed to my exhausted and belatedly outraged mind, into those of an obituary: Where had she been born? . . . Had she attended or had she been graduated from Sarah Lawrence? . . . What was her first movie role? . . . and I was able to continue to answer these questions politely until one voice inquired expressionlessly: Are you her next of kin? . . . and I had snapped back: No, *you* are! which didn't mean anything and wasn't even insulting.

It was at that point, with the wan first glow of dawn showing through the east windows of the living room, that sickly light so many revelers and drunks and good-time Charlies and overeager party girls have been forced to notice with sinking heart, that pale signal that the party is over, the glamour of darkness is fleeing and all the drudgery and problems momentarily shaken off during the party are lying out there in the predawn, waiting . . . at this point I concluded that I had better go upstairs to my room and take at least a short nap. Pauline had crept up to her room some time before.

As I stepped into the hall and was crossing to the stairway Bruno burst out of the entrance to the dining room and began his bounding dance around me. Mrs. Purvis came with her usual tentative dignity along behind him.

I had never seen her any way except starched and coiffed, cool and immaculate. Now her black hair fell in a braid past her shoulders, and she wore a gray wrapper. She squinted at me; that had never happened before either. Her gaze had always been calm, cool and respectful. She must wear contact lenses, I said to myself with a kind of dazed reflectiveness, and now she hasn't got them in. Squinting, she began apologetically as Bruno sniffed my shoes, "Forgive me for—I hadn't time to dress because— so silly but—cars coming back so late—the telephone constantly ringing—I just wondered if anyone needed anything? An early breakfast? I should have dressed, of course, but something said to me to—well—hurry, hurry out here and see if I was perhaps wanted?" She squinted apologetically at me once more.

I exhaled slowly and looked across at her: her posture seemed to have been left behind with her starched clothes; she seemed slightly bent, hunched. "Edna—" I had always without thinking called her "Mrs. Purvis" before— "something serious has happened. Something very serious. To Axie." I would have said "Miss Reed" before. Edna's face drained of blood and of expression. "She's in the hospital. She took a fall, well a very bad fall at the party, and she's in Southampton Hospital. It's serious. I'm afraid it's very serious."

She muttered something and turned swiftly back toward her room. "What?" I called after her.

"I'll be at the hospital," she said slurringly, as though answering my question was an irrelevancy, and she disappeared.

"They won't let you see her," I called after her, but that to her was an irrelevancy, too.

I roamed uncertainly up the wide stairway and at the

top turned left. On my right, windows looked out across the tiny balcony to the bay and the ocean. What a bright, beautiful, cheery morning had dawned! Just gorgeous. I trudged on to the door of her room, paused, and uncertainly, unwillingly, peered in. Her nightgown, something white and filmy, had been laid diagonally upon her bed by Edna. Two tiny lamps burned on her dressing table, where silver-handled hairbrushes waited. A light ocean breeze slowly inflated the draperies and then let them fall back into place again, and then slowly, gently blew them once more a little way into the room: it was like breathing, as though the room were breathing, breathing for Alexandra.

I went on, turning left again and down the hall to my room, solid, foursquare, Edwardian. Slowly I began to undress, get out of this tuxedo, and this damn dress shirt, and these damn studs, and these bloody patent-leather evening slippers.

Axie had given them to me, and they weren't my style; I wore them because they had come from her.

I slid them off and, in underpants, collapsed back on the high bed.

Fatigue started to flow out of my back and my neck and my legs.

This seemed to be—was—the first unhappy time I had ever spent in this house. When she was still a girl—fourteen, fifteen—Axie had blasted her way into my little-boy life by teaching me to swim in the cove, to sail in the bay, finally to catch waves in the ocean. Obviously this little boy cousin of hers allowed her to rehearse her maternal instincts, instincts which were as it turned out to have virtually no other outlet. Some teenage girls rode horses; Axie mothered, or rather older-sistered me. She was quick and blond, a blonde who turned golden brown in the sun and not beet red, a long golden quick blonde, big-eyed and laughing and with already in her voice a trace of the huskiness which became her trademark, a quick coordinated skillful young girl teaching a little boy how to deal with the water which lay all around them.

My family lived on the North Shore of Long Island, much closer to the city, but Axie, having once laid eyes on me at an extended family gathering in New York, a very extended family gathering because our consanguine relationship was not close, having once spotted me, she snatched me away from the North Shore when the spirit moved her, put me into the second-best guest room at Portals, and taught me these skills.

Of course I fell in love with her, what else could I do? And this emotional lock she had on me went through many mutations and modifications and developments and curtailments between my being seven years old and my now being forty-three years old. But it was never severed, and by now, never could be.

Except of course by death.

11

Within a half hour of learning of the accident, Edna, starchy and upright, had somehow crept past the attendants in the dim, almost silent intensive care unit and made her way into Axie's cubicle. She stood very still in the dim room looking down upon her mistress, who was unconscious. Alexandra Reed seemed to have become a prone body dominated by a system of tubes. A tube led out of an incision under her right arm; a tube had been jabbed into her right shoulder—intravenous feeding; tubes went through her nose, her mouth, where a machine was pumping air through the tube into her lungs.

All this Edna could bear. But the final touch, final indignity, caused her to come close to fainting. Alexandra, her beloved Axie, was tied to this bed, her wrists bound to the metal strips running along the sides of the bed.

Edna was blindly beginning to untie these when the nurse found her, and led her away. "She must not be untied," the nurse said not unkindly when she had learned who Edna was, "she might reach up involuntarily and knock the respirator away. Then she would suffocate."

Edna went to the waiting room and sat there, and sat there. She was sitting there at ten that Sunday morning when Spyro Talouris burst in. "How is she?" he demanded.

Edna looked up and after a pause murmured, "She's tied, tied to the bed. Her eyes are closed."

Spyro, still dressed for sailing, went swiftly out again and to the door of the intensive care unit. The male attendant there recognized him as one of the rich shipping Talourises, but didn't know whether this was the one who ran the company or the one who was in government.

"I've got to see Alexandra Reed," Spyro said in his level voice, his level gaze, blue-eyed, coming out of his wind-burned face, "I'm her brother-in-law and her best friend."

"No one can see her. Doctor's orders. Sorry."

"I have to see her," Spyro went on as though the

other had not spoken, "and here is something I want to contribute to the hospital welfare fund," slipping him a hundred-dollar bill.

The attendant glanced at the bill and then looked back at Spyro. Then he said, "You won't say anything about this visit, will you? All kinds of people want in there—friends, reporters, even a photographer. I'm glad *I'm* not a movie star, after seeing this."

"Mm. Where is she?"

The attendant escorted him to Axie's cubicle, put his finger to his lips, and left.

Spyro stood motionless looking down at her. He willed for her eyes to open. He stood there, willing her to return to consciousness, and after a while Axie's eyes began to flutter—later he would not know whether he stood there waiting for five minutes or twenty-five minutes—and she looked up at him.

Axie could not move, and she could not speak; she could only gaze up at him.

"It's me," he said in a husky undertone. "You wanted me here, didn't you?" He went on gazing at her. "I knew you did, and so I'm here. I've always had strength for you. I have something to put in your hand." Axie slowly was able to turn her left hand palm up. "It's a coin," Spyro said in his husky whisper, "from the Grove of Hippocrates on Samos. Remember? Just hold it. You remember the day I found it there. Keep on holding it." His voice began to quaver, but he forced himself on. "That's my strength you're holding. That's Greece and that's the discovery of medicine by a Greek. You will get better. You are Greek by marriage. Don't think about any divorce; that was just a piece of paper. You are one of us. You are a Talouris, a Greek, and you are going to hold that coin from the Grove of Hippocrates and get well. I know you are. You have my strength now."

Then, since he was on the verge of crying and since Spyro had never been seen to cry by anyone since he was a very small child, he turned and left the cubicle.

Then, gathering up the protesting Edna, he drove over to Portals.

12

It was an August morning very much like the preceding one, same sunlight pouring steadily down, same breezy salubrious optimistic atmosphere, and Portals looked very much the same: Bruno exploring the edge of lawn bordering the bed of rosebushes, Edna bringing late breakfast on trays to the East Porch for Pauline Marsh and me. She and I happened to be dressed very much as we had been the day before. We sat in the same wicker chairs. The only change was that the long wicker couch was empty.

Spyro had been out in the kitchen, talking confidingly to Edna. Spyro always established a rapport with housekeepers, maids, chauffeurs, gardeners and the garbage man: with people socially and economically more his equal he tended to be edgy, hard to know.

Now he came out onto the porch with a glass of orange juice and sat down on the empty couch. "What do we do now?" he demanded.

"Spyro, this is Pauline Marsh."

"What do we do now?" he repeated his question to me.

There was no point in trying to force the introduction, and I was going to give up on it when Spyro suddenly turned his glare on her. "You work for a newspaper?" She nodded. "You're the bitch who took that photograph." Pauline returned his stare. Then Spyro turned once again to me. "What do we do now?"

I told him what I had done so far—talking to the press and many friends, talking to her agent; to Douglas Shore, her director; to relatives. Axie's parents had both died when a plane they had chartered crashed approaching Nantucket Island in a fog five years before and so in a sense I and Spyro and Spyro's brother, Lambros, Axie's ex-husband, were the closest people in the world to her.

We were, and yet in another sense, the closest people in the world to Axie were her fans. She had a particularly personal impact on the public, as certain stars do. People *identified* with Axie in her characterizations. She represented something for them, their ideal of a certain kind of woman, free and independent and outspoken and even wild, but also with a streak of vulnerability. She had played that kind of role over and over, and the public never seemed to tire of her in it. This public, therefore, was close to Axie too, had a kind of stake in her fate, had it by virtue of caring so much about her, or at least the Alexandra Reed they believed her to be. This little village of Water Mill in the Town of Southampton was sufficiently out in the country so that fans rarely came to this house. They knew vaguely that she lived "out on Long Island" and that was usually all they knew.

The telephone rang again and Edna told me it was the hospital calling. I raced into the living room and grabbed the telephone. It was Dr. LaBrianca.

"Your cousin is now in our intensive care unit. She is being fed intravenously, and she seems to be holding her own. The whole question is whether she will sink further into shock and go into a coma. If that should happen, then her condition will be very grave. But, if that does *not* happen, if she is able to resist it, and in a situation like this, she can only fight, you might say subconsciously, she may recover." He paused, and then finished quietly, "It really depends on what her gut feeling is about life."

13

Axie rose up from the depths from time to time into consciousness. She was no longer aboard a boat now, but was in the sea itself, deep in the depths of the sea, the Mediterranean surely, for it was bluish and crystalline, with no sense of coldness about it, but instead just a heaviness, the heaviness of the sea, the Mediterranean or really the Aegean, this heavy bluish sea above and all around her, heavy, so heavy. But from time to time her body would float gently upward, and she would even emerge on the surface and find herself in this tent, but then she would remember that it was not a tent, it was a hospital cubicle and something had struck her physically, and she had been at that party and Nick Reed was staying at Portals.

Her body seemed to be bound everywhere, and tubes, these tubes running into her head through her nose and mouth and down her throat. Also, she could not move her hands. Some strange machine just above her mouth was pumping out air rhythmically. It was pumping air into her, but not enough air. She was not getting enough air. But there was nothing whatever that she could do about that.

The heaviness and the exhaustion began to make her sink again, to drift down into the bluish sea again.

That was Spyro who had been here, not here in the depths of the sea, but here in her hospital cubicle, for she now inhabited both of these places simultaneously. Spyro had stood beside her bed and offered her his strength, and yes he had given her a coin, an old Greek coin from Samos and in fact she could still feel it in her left hand, feel the oldness of it, the wornness of it.

This coin was associated with Hippocrates, father of medicine, and with Spyro Talouris who had found it, Spyro who had conquered youthful weakness in himself and was strong, Spyro who had come to her bedside to give her his strength, Spyro who loved her. Oh yes, he loved her.

Axie had never admitted this to herself before. After all, she had been married to his brother. Lambros was older, Lambros she had only really gotten to know shortly before marrying him. She had grown up with her exact contemporary Spyro, been in school with him.

As a little boy, he had been sort of buck-toothed and clownish, but then he began to grow into the look of a young, reddish wolf, lean and predatory.

They had been seventeen years old, she and Spyro, students in a private school outside Boston called Purcell Academy, and one Saturday they had gone on a bicycle ride together a little way into the countryside. Finally they had stopped to rest, wandered into a field, a meadow of high grass. It was autumn, evocative scented New England autumn; there was cool sunlight and softness in the air. Spyro took her hand to help her over one of those low stony New England walls, and Axie felt the lean strength of that tanned, freckled hand, that self-made athlete's hand, and there sprang unbidden, unexpected into her mind a calculation: if she pretended to stumble now, he wouldn't be able to do anything except catch her in those taut arms— she could suddenly feel with certitude that this was what he urgently wanted to do—and that wide mouth which curved so rarely but so invitingly into a smile would come against hers, and he would be struggling, his mouth and his sex, to enter into her, enter at last, the momentum of those years of companionship suddenly thrusting into Eros, the god of sexual love, tagalong buddy-buddies transformed magically into lovers, there in the long grass in the meadow in the autumn.

But Axie had not stumbled. She had always been as sure-footed as a mountain chamois, but she was already sensing her powers as an actress, and she could have made him believe that she truly stumbled, and he would have caught her in his arms, and he would have kissed her just the way she imagined, and his hands would have roamed her body, and they would have slid down together into the long grass.

But Axie had not stumbled. There was some deep inner impediment. Something blocked her from violating their friendship that day. Oh, he loved her. And she loved him, too. Few people did or ever would, he was too abrasive for that, too self-made tough. But she had known him always, and she loved him, and she was drawn to the feel of him, of his mouth and his arms and his stomach and his sex, everything . . .

But she had not stumbled. They had been close, close

companions, platonic, and so Plato and not Eros had won the day, some deep inner imperative had said *no,* he is not for you nor you for him, and if you do this today your friendship will be shot to smithereens, and the sexual link is not right and will not last and will do harm. Such a coupling, you and Spyro, is not in destiny's plan. You can do it; stumble toward him now, and it is all over, he will react exactly as you foresee.

Some force implying all this within her kept her moving with supple smoothness up and over the stone wall.

That was perhaps why he was still devoted to her, and she to him: because she had not stumbled into his arms that day, and they had not then and never afterward learned the feel and the passion of one another's bodies. Withheld sexuality was the steely bond between them; having sacrificed sex they could not—ever—sacrifice companionship. To do so would have made the other sacrifice such a terrible, ludicrous waste. They were bound together for life by mutual withheld sexual love.

Spyro Spyro, she repeated inwardly, as she seemed to spin slowly in her bed and in this sea, slowly turning—in a whirlpool? Being sucked downward? Spyro for strength. Such a mean man, so rude so much of the time. So unkind, no compassion, not on the surface anyway. Spyro . . . the Greek islands; their Greek island, the Talouris family's own Greek island, Paxos . . . what a fragment of beauty. Would she see it ever again?

Well I have seen it in the past, she asserted bravely to herself, I have seen it, lived among those magic phosphorescent lanes many times for many months, when that unbelievable full Grecian moon makes the white walls and lanes glow like the corridors of paradise.

If I am dying, it is not before I have lived.

14

At Portals, Spyro, Pauline and I had moved into the square, high-ceilinged living room with its many French doors, so that I could be closer to the telephone, which continued to ring every few minutes.

When Spyro Talouris was angry with someone, there was no point, no possibility of deflecting him short of shooting him in the head.

At one point when the conversation flagged and Pauline tried to move into the vacuum— "What was that school like that Axie went to with . . . you . . ." venturing to address Spyro directly . . . "outside Boston? Was it—" Spyro had simply stood up and strolled over to the fireplace, looking up at an oil portrait above it. It was a painting of Axie, done when she was about twenty-eight years old. In it she was seated, wearing a shimmering evening dress, her dark blond hair falling to her shoulders, portrayed here in a serious mood, the large green-gray-blue eyes gazing thoughtfully into the distance, gazing perhaps a little unhappily, and with the dignity of unhappiness. The overall sheen of the portrait was golden, with blue and green highlights and undertones.

Pauline went onto the offensive. "You have to look at that painting, do you? Never seen it before?"

His back to her, he didn't turn. Finally he said sourly, "You ask questions all the time?" There was an unpleasant silence. "And take photos of anybody anywhere they are?"

"It's my job," she said simply. "It's what I'm paid to do."

He drew a noisy breath. "Myself, I'd be a two-bit whore first, if I were you."

Pauline recoiled—it was as though she had been slapped in the face with a dead fish—and fumbled for a retort, any retort.

"Lay off her," I said to Spyro. "What difference does the photo make anyway? It's terrible taste, I grant you"— I had no inclination to protect Pauline Marsh; this was candor day at Portals— "but it doesn't change anything."

Now she'll get up and leave the room and go upstairs and pack and leave Portals.

That projection of mine greatly underestimated Pauline. Axie's dramatic accident was news, big news for August. Other photographers were already out in the Hamptons photographing the marquee and the spot where Axie had fallen, photographing the outside of Southampton Hospital; reporters were seeking interviews here and there and everywhere around here associated with Alexandra.

Axie was certainly a famous actress, if now on the verge of becoming a has-been. Normally even such a dramatic accident might have excited less interest in the media: but this was August, the journalistic dog days; Washington was empty; New York City was somnolent, its leading personalities, many of them, out here on the East End; there was no war, there were no peace negotiations, no riots, no epidemic: it was, therefore, journalistically speaking, the season of gossip, the tried and true—or false— stories about "celebrities." Axie willy-nilly was one of these, and she had done something more sensational than adultery or taking drugs. The terrible sudden shattering of her body and her edging toward death were therefore prime gossip, juicy morsels of gossip for a hungry press.

It was disgusting for me and for those of us who loved Axie, and the peculiar fact that a prime purveyor of gossip was staying here in the house left me, at least, feeling bollixed.

I did not see how I could throw her out, exactly. It wasn't my house; I hadn't invited her in. Of course she would go, that was the only logical and civilized thing to do.

But of course she would not go. She was not being civilized; she was a reporter on a story.

So she sat there, and Spyro insulted her whenever he remembered she was there and could think of an insult, and Pauline said little and noted everything.

15

This is what Pauline Marsh dictated into her recorder later that day:

Axie Reed is in intensive care, and it's touch and go. She looked beautiful just before she fell, and on the ground she looked like a stricken deer.

She's alone in the world, and she's got a lot of people who love her. Weird. The cousin here, Nicholas Reed, is completely devoted to her. Otherwise he's a kind of detached type. Never married. Now on leave of absence from the University of Vermont. Historian, specializing on Russia. Wrote two popular biographies, one on Nijinsky and one on Maria Feodorovna, the last tsar of Russia's mother. Made money with them. Also inherited some, I take it. No threadbare academic he. Speaking of money, Axie must be kind of loaded, and I guess he's probably her heir. This is not occurring to him right now. Everybody around here is acting as though the world is coming to an end.

Then there's Spyro Talouris. Spyro Talouris is a shit. Younger son of Stamos Talouris, the Greek shipping tycoon. Spoiled rotten. Mean as a rattlesnake. His older brother, Lambros, now runs the family shipping business, and Spyro wants to be in Congress or the Senate or the White House. Over my dead body. Right now, he does special assignments for the State Department. Diplomacy. What a hoot. Diplomacy! Spyro Talouris?

He is the subject of my next profile, after I finish this Reed one. It will be the hatchet job to end all hatchet jobs. He won't be able to sue me, because he's a public figure, and he'll never be able to prove malice. Me, feel malice toward Spyro Talouris? Don't be silly. I could kill him, that's all.

The worst is, the bastard's attractive. About five ten, hundred and seventy, lean, athletic, sunburned, quick movements, sharp glance.

Spyro Talouris—funny, I can't bring myself to call him by his first name only; to do it would grate on me, strange—Spyro Talouris has spent all his summers out here in the Hamptons since birth, and he and Axie are exactly the same age and ran into each other when they were building sand castles on the beach when they were two, or something like that. Not only that, they went to the same Quaker school in New York City and then the same Wasp private school in Massachusetts. They grew up in lockstep.

Note for Spyro piece: His father, Stamos, sent him, a Greek Orthodox boy, to first a Quaker school and then a Protestant school. Wanted him completely integrated into American society.

Greek Orthodox or even Roman Catholic were too special. Reason: Spyro—what the hell, I'll call him that—was designed by the father to be the political son.

Then there's Lambros. He used to be Axie's husband. He isn't here yet. The senior Talourises haven't arrived yet either.

Edna, the maid or housekeeper or whatever, also worships Axie. So does Bruno, the dog.

That's how she made her success as an actress, I see now. I've seen quite a few of her movies and caught her on the stage in two plays. Very effective. But no great actress. It's this hold she gets on people, magnetism, she's got it in life, and she's got it professionally. Striking-looking, of course, but how many good-looking women were there in Hollywood when she was starting out? A thousand? Ten thousand? What she had and has is something compelling, something people don't want to let go of.

Now everyone around here is petrified that it's going to be taken away from them by this crazy accident.

Note: Get all possible medical details from Dr.

LaBrianca. Interview nurses, attendants in intensive care.

Right now, here at Portals, it's background time.

The school in Massachusetts, Purcell Academy. Background I got from an Axie-Spyro classmate in Washington. Axie was the queen of the school, because she didn't want to be. Today I found a yearbook in the living room and already at this school Axie had those long, slender, beautiful legs, and that mane of hair, and I'm sure she had that look in her eye, that gleam, which said that she was going beyond them, somewhere else, somewhere better. She was like a lady eagle perched at this Purcell Academy for a few years, and then she'd spread her wings and—look out! All the boys were fascinated, and most of the girls really were too, secretly. They couldn't call her stuck-up, could they, because to tell you the truth all of them sound stuck-up to me, but usually so polite you'd never know it. They were the kind of kids that when one of them had a father who won the Nobel Prize for Physics and another student said, "Isn't that your father?" he answers, "Yup." Understated. Never boast. Brush off praise. Stiff upper lip. British, don't you know. Ugh. Well thank God I didn't go there. Anyway, there was Axie, and she was flamboyant even then and too outgoing and her stride was too long, and the girls watched her, and the boys were mesmerized.

And Spyro Talouris watched all this. He himself can't have been popular at the Purcell Academy or anywhere else. He's Mr. Abrasive now; then I suppose he was just ignored, put down, snubbed. In schools like that nobody cares how much money your family has. There's nothing there to spend money on. If your name is Rockefeller, they would at least know who you are, not care, but know. With Spyro Talouris they wouldn't even know. "Talouris? What kind of a name is that?" "Greek." "Oh." End of conversation.

And Axie, the queen of the school, would have been close to him through thick and thin. That's the kind of woman she is now, and that's the kind of girl she would have been then. Nobody likes my friend Spyro? Then I'll make him my best friend and defend him every moment of every day.

Well, out of all that Spyro developed tough, very tough, and not caring what anybody thinks of him outside his tight little circle.

He sure as hell doesn't care about me. But wait till he sees what I write about him.

But first I've got to get more, much more, about Alexandra Reed. And fast. Her story won't be hot a week from now.

16

Axie rose slowly out of the depths again, up all the way to the surface. The strange machine aimed at the tube in her mouth still rhythmically pumped air into her lungs, but still not enough, not enough. With all the parts of her which had been broken, with the incredible fatigue, like the whole weight of the sea, pressing down upon her, she must have air, adequate air at least, if she was to live.

And she wasn't getting it.

She still held the small smooth coin of Samos in her left hand. With the tubes in her nose and mouth, she could scarcely move her head, but she was able to raise it a little from the pillow and actually look down at the small grayish disc, a little gray disc which could have bought you something, an elixir perhaps, on the island of Samos a few thousand years ago, an elixir from Hippocrates himself, to mend your body and lift your spirit.

Next to this left hand of hers, bound to the frame of the bed, she saw a button, a buzzer, pinned to the sheet. Axie was able to move her hand over and press it, wondering what if anything might thereby appear. Nothing whatever would have surprised her: a genie, a Nubian slave, her guardian angel.

A woman in white with a white cap came quietly into the room: a nurse, prosaically enough—and thank God for it—a nurse who looked to be a normal, competent American.

Axie looked up pleadingly at her and tried to convey through her great eyes—critics had often commented on how expressive they were in close-ups—to convey: *I'm not getting enough air.* The nurse appeared to cock her head slightly, as Bruno often did when he did not, quite, comprehend an order of hers.

Then the most basic kind of theater came suddenly to her rescue: mime. With her left fingers, despite the wrist lashed to the bed, she pantomimed writing.

"You want to write something," commented the nurse.

Axie nodded her head tightly and desperately.

The nurse went out and returned with a pad and pencil, placing the pencil in Axie's left hand and the pad beneath it. But tied as she was, Axie could not manage to make any marks on the paper. This time she turned her eyes in pleading, in anguish, once more upon the nurse, and this time the nurse could read the message. "You want me to untie your hand."

Axie simply went on gazing pleadingly at her.

"I don't know . . ." the nurse began hesitantly, "the doctor wants your hands bound." Axie's gaze never wavered; it just pleaded. "Well, just for a moment, while you write whatever it is. But. *Do not touch, you must not touch the respirator.*"

Axie nodded tensely to this.

Then her left hand was untied. A tingling of relief then rose up in her: untied, only one of her two hands, but at least one of them! Until this taste of freedom, she had not realized how punishing this confinement had been. One hand free. Just for now, but what a release.

Then on the pad, clumsily, drunkenly, she scrawled in childish block letters: I'M NOT GETTING ENOUGH AIR.

The nurse read the message, nodded, it seemed, absently adjusted the respirator minutely, and then, like a prison warden, retied Axie's left wrist to the frame of the bed. She straightened the pillow, gazed at her for a moment, and then quietly went out.

She had made no comment about Axie's desperate message.

After a while Axie realized: She can't make any comment; there is no comment to make. They can't give me any more air. The machine is pumping plenty of air. It's me, my lungs. They can't absorb any more; something's wrong with them. They can't take in any more. It's not the machine, it's me. I'm not functioning right. The people here can't do anything about it.

I am not getting enough air. And I may die of it.

Her mind began to drift back over this life, which she now seemed close to the point of losing, so suddenly, so inexplicably losing.

I have been an actress all of my adult life: in fact I was only twenty years old when somebody first paid me to act—1951, off Broadway, worse than that, down in a cellar in the West Village, and my first line was, "Is there a bus station around here?"

And now here I am, not quite fifty and everything has shot along professionally ever since I said that line. A man sitting in the middle of that tiny audience, Douglas Shore, heard something in my voice when I said that line, liked the way I came striding on stage before I said it, and decided to take an interest in me.

So I became a real actress and famous and successful, and it has all shot past me in a blur, and maybe I never should have been an actress, maybe I should have been a real wife and a mother and done volunteer work at the Red Cross.

But even as these thoughts flowed through Alexandra's head, a contradictory and dominating voice beneath her thoughts was unanswerably communicating to her: You had no choice at all, and you know that you didn't; you had to be an actress, just as Bruno has to be a German shepherd. Could Bruno have turned out to be a poodle? Well then, how could you have been anything but an actress?

And this deep-within countervoice calmed Axie, and as she slipped into unconsciousness once again, the weight of the sea pressing down upon her seemed a little less onerous, somewhat less crushing.

THREE

17

Around noon I drove to the hospital to meet Dr. La-
Brianca. He had just been in to examine Axie, and when
I asked to see her, he looked at me dubiously. Then he
said, after drawing a slow breath, "Well, if you insist. But
I wouldn't advise it. There's nothing you will be able to
see. She's not awake, and we have the respirator and intravenous apparatus in place, and it isn't . . . well, relatives
don't like to see that. There's nothing you can do for her
right now. Her color isn't—good, she's well, she's very
pale, sallow-looking. She's a woman who is in critical
condition, so what can one expect? She looks frankly like
what she is: a very, very seriously ill and injured woman.

We're doing everything, as I told you, and now it's what her body can do to respond, and . . . on how she . . . values life."

"How long is this going to go on?" I asked in a low voice.

"That we don't know. Her platelet count could begin to improve at any time, and her other life signs pick up. Or else, she might hang there like this for days. Not weeks, days. There will have to be a change, one way or the other, within I would say three or four days. She cannot remain longer in the state she is now in. The body cannot for very long sustain this."

"The telephone calls are beginning to taper off, at least," I said irrelevantly, as though this were a hopeful sign.

"Yes, well we've had reporters coming around here, and photographers. Of course they can't get anywhere near her, and we can just say she is still critical."

"We've got a journalist staying at Axie's house," I said. "From her, I get the impression this is Sunday's story, and maybe Monday's and Tuesday's. But after that some other story, similar in some way, will happen. Some other actress or sports star will have a crisis, and the press will more or less forget about this—our situation here. Un-less . . . well . . . unless there is some . . . dramatic change . . ."

"Where may I reach you, in case I need to?" Dr. LaBrianca inquired. "I suppose you have to go back to work tomorrow?"

"No. I'm on leave of absence from the university, University of Vermont. So I'll stay here, stay on at Axie's house, while I'm needed. Other, well, relatives, in a manner of speaking, will be arriving. Axie's ex-husband. And *his* parents, her ex-parents-in-law."

Dr. LaBrianca looked bemused by this category of relationship.

"Yeah, I know," I said drily. "Strange relationship, or nonrelationship. Well, as somebody already said, the rich are different from you and me."

Dr. LaBrianca seemed to be relaxing after a strenuous professional weekend. He cocked a look at me. "Aren't you, well, wealthy, too? None of my business, I—"

"Sure it's your business, why not? The family's foremost member is in your hands. Anything you want to know about us, just ask. No, I'm not rich at all. A college teacher, rich? But I get fifteen thousand dollars a year from money I inherited and invested, and the university pays me forty, and I've had two modest best-selling books. So, I am I guess what they call 'comfortable.'"

"No family, children?"

"No," I said.

I was not the domestic type, never had been, right from childhood, even though my parents had had, as far as I could tell, a workable marriage. I myself had felt stifled in their house, subconsciously vowing that if I ever escaped from this airless domestic atmosphere of marriage and children, I would never again get trapped in it. And I hadn't.

Axie was like that too. Born into different branches of the family, we had that in common. Axie instinctively and viscerally resisted a conventional marriage and family. She had told me so. She didn't know why this was, exactly, but she knew it was a fundamental part of her.

She was not at all sure motherhood went with a career as an actress, especially a successful and busy actress going on location to places like Kenya or Japan. She had married, to be sure, but it had been a very open, traveling, separated-for-extended-periods kind of marriage, and that had been the only kind she had wanted, had dared to enter into. Like me, she feared that the tentacles of a conventional marriage might constrict and eventually choke her.

Axie, nevertheless, loved children because she loved people, and she treated the new Talouris generation, Spyro's and Lambros's children, as individuals of great interest to her. People fascinated Axie, and children were definitely people. Especially since she herself was preeminently one of those people who had never for an instant lost touch with their own childhood.

She remembered how it felt to build sand castles on the beach and desperately struggle to construct last-minute moats and thickened walls to protect them from destruction by the inexorable incoming waves; she remembered Popsicles and how good they tasted when you were eight going on nine; she could recollect the intoxication that had coursed through her as the family car, a black Buick sedan, approached the house in Water Mill for the first time each spring after a gloomy winter in Brooklyn Heights, and then her first sighting of the ocean each season. She could still experience the almost choking esctasy as, each season, she drew near the ocean itself and could smell its tang and hear its cushioned, distantly mighty crash, still there from last summer and the summer before and the one before that, the faithful, fateful eternal muffled explosion of the surf against the hard-packed whitish sand of the East End.

Axie never had and never could lose touch with any of those sense memories; her nerves still tingled with the sensations of childhood, as vivid as anything in her life had been since.

18

Back at Portals, I was sitting, more or less sprawling, in
the white wicker chair on the East Porch. I didn't usually
sprawl, but Axie's ordeal was slowly, as though drop by
drop, draining the morale out of me. If only I could *do*
something! It was this enforced inactivity which was draining me. Answering the telephone wasn't enough, not nearly
enough.

Then I heard her voice, quite clearly, in my ear. "Go
for a swim in the cove, you oaf. Don't just sprawl there."
I heard her penetrating, compelling voice say this into my
ear. Was I going to be haunted by her voice forever, if I
never heard it again in life? Were delusions going to replace
the vivid reality of Axie Reed?

I pulled myself out of the chair and went up to my
room, put on some swimming trunks and the blue terry-
cloth bathrobe which she always hung in my room when
I visited Portals. Then I went down through the house,
out across the lawn to the dock, stood gazing at the mysterious green-gray water swaying faintly there, and then
dived in. How right she had been; it felt great. Then I
reflected: *How right she had been?* What did *that* mean? That
had not been Axie's voice; that had come up from my
subconscious.

A certain profound confusion was seeping into my
mind as this ordeal of my cousin's lengthened and didn't

change, just went on: Alexandra Reed is in the intensive care unit in critical condition. That was what the medical people in charge said, over and over, and that's all they would or could say.

I was a good swimmer, thanks to Axie, so I stroked easily out toward the center of Mecox Bay, turned and then backstroked back toward the dock. My backstroke was good. I must have looked as though I was thoroughly enjoying myself, with not a care in the world.

You can't hear voices when you're swimming that way, and it was only when I drifted to a stop quite close to the dock that I heard an exasperated voice yelling for obviously the third or tenth time, "Hey! You!"

It was the director, the man who had "discovered" Axie, Douglas Shore. Yes, of course he would turn up. That he had even got here before Lambros did not surprise me.

"Oh hi," I called back. "I'll be right out."

When I climbed up the little home-made ladder onto the dock, he asked carefully, "Have a good swim?"

Now Douglas Shore was not really an actor, in fact not an actor at all. He had to my knowledge only played one role professionally in his life. But he was a director, and so he was in a way all actors, and all actresses too; in any case, he had full control of his voice. Therefore it did not, as he delivered the line "Have a good swim?" convey even an undertone of sarcasm or anger; the line had just been carefully delivered, leaving me to add the inferences.

"How are you?" I asked, self-possessed and with a slight grin, taking care to ignore his question.

His rather large blue eyes widened for an instant, and I saw his rejoinder forming, *"How could I be with Axie on the brink of death?"* but I didn't let him deliver it: "And how are all of us?" I went on, "how could we be?"

He seemed to wilt there in the sun in front of me. Douglas Shore was rather short, rather broad-shouldered, and quite sensitive. Suddenly I thought: You look a lot like Stamos Talouris, except that you're sensitive, and he's a pile-driver.

"No," he finally muttered, "I couldn't bear to have some operator at the switchboard over there tell me that Axie was . . . was . . ."

"Still critical," I swiftly let drop, knowing that with those words I was relieving for him a breathless suspense: there were a couple of worse words.

"What can I do?" he said quietly.

"That's just it: you can't do one damn thing, and neither can I. That's why I just took that swim, trying to work off some of the frustration."

His eyes lighted up for a second, and I saw that, now, having known me fairly well for thirty years, he had suddenly decided that he liked me.

I decided, as I wiped myself off with a towel there on the dock, that I liked him too.

He had been the great professional influence in Axie's career: she had always been, in her own way, devoted to him. So how was it that I had held him at arm's length all these years? Snobbery? Was I some kind of snob? I had never thought so, never dreamed it. But wasn't that at the root of my sort of bypassing Douglas Shore whenever we met, because of his differentness?

Had this differentness been enough for me to keep him at a distance? How superficial *was* I? What kind of person, after all, was Nicholas Reed, who, in a sense like Axie, had fallen into good fortune, and had never had to struggle, not really, not viscerally, not life and death, for what he wanted in life?

Douglas Shore, standing a little uncertainly before me, in white flannel pants and a blue blazer—his notion of how people should dress in the fashionable Hamptons—Douglas Shore had had to claw his way to professional fulfillment, from Jersey City to Greenwich Village to Beverly Hills. And he had wanted urgently to marry Alexandra Reed, and she would not. Nothing had come easily; everything had to be first dreamed of and then agonizingly struggled for. Much of his dream he had achieved; he was a respected director with quite a few successes on both stage and screen. But he was not a top director either commercially or in terms of prestige, and he had not gotten Axie. He still loved her, of course. And she was still devoted to him, had always accepted any role he offered her, believing that he knew best. But she would not marry him.

"Come up to the house," I said with a kind of sigh, a little wearily; before the swim I had felt tense; now I felt let down.

We walked rather slowly across the wide, smooth, gently sloping lawn and Douglas finally said, "Will I be able to see her?"

After a silence, I answered, "You wouldn't want to," not realizing how that would sound to him. He froze in his tracks and turned his face with a look of spreading horror toward me.

"Oh no, no," I blurted. "She isn't *disfigured* or anything like that. There's nothing external that you can see. It's all *internal,* all the injuries. I just mean, there are all these tubes and the intravenous feeding and all that. Plus she's, well, she's asleep most of the time."

Not moving, he continued to study me. Finally, he asked flatly, "Asleep? Is it sleep?"

"Well . . . I don't know . . . she's unconscious . . ."

"Does that mean a coma?"

"I don't think so. Not . . . not . . . yet . . ."

He looked at me some more and then we both turned and slogged on toward the house.

I got Douglas established in the big cool living room. I persuaded him to take off his blazer. I made a vodka and tonic for him, a strong one, and another for me. It was probably going to be a long and pointless day, a day of waiting.

And so it turned out to be, the first of a string of such days, and I soon began to learn that waiting was the most terrible thing in the world. I would much rather have been in intensive interrogation by the KGB, far preferable would have been a regime of brainwashing at the hands of murky Communists somewhere; how lucky were migrant workers toiling in relentless sun down a row of lettuce for a pittance a day; how fortunate were street cleaners and convicts who worked at polishing toilets.

But Douglas and I could do nothing. I still handled the occasional phone call. Pauline Marsh had borrowed my car and, while she had not said so, I knew she was scouring the area for "background." Spyro had gone home to the Talouris house on the beach. Edna had gone to pray at the Catholic church, and Bruno, although he had accepted Axie's many earlier absences calmly, today continually went from room to room, floor to floor, out to search the rose garden, the lawn, the dock, then back in to search the floors again.

In the living room Douglas Shore and I had to do the worst thing anybody in these circumstances is asked to do: wait.

Doug was gazing up at the golden portrait of Axie over the fireplace. He had not seen it often before; Axie

tended to see her professional friends in her apartment in
New York, keeping Portals for family and longtime friends.
None of us was in the theatrical world. She had found
long ago that these two groups did not mix well, and that
the members of each group were happier to see her in their
own context. Out here Axie was one of the Brooklyn
Heights and Southampton Reeds; in there she was the star
of *The Provincetown Story,* and the numerous other films
and plays which had followed this first hit. She could of
course switch in and out of these two disparate categories
we placed her in in the wink of an eye; she was always
acting, playing to different audiences, always performing,
and always, or nearly always, putting her heart into it.

"That painting there," Douglas began, gazing ana-
lytically up at it. "How old do you suppose she was when
it was painted?"

"Her late twenties, I think."

"That's Axie after she'd become a star. That's the Axie
her career made her, isn't it? But that's not the girl I first
knew.

"The Axie I met was hardly more than a schoolgirl,
kind of proper. You felt you were keeping her from her
homework. But out of her came all kinds of tiny signals,
little hints and glimpses of something underneath, someone getting out little signals that said underneath there's—
well, there's that lady up there on the wall. Beautiful.
Glittering. Big. Big eyes, wide mouth. Tall. Striding. A
strider. And the voice . . ." He seemed to sink into a rev-
erie, and I felt it best to leave him there as long as he
wanted; he would momentarily have lost himself in recollections and have obliterated for a period the onerousness
he and I bore together: the waiting.

"See, the thing with Axie was that the moment I first

saw her, in some little cellar in the Village walking on in some dumb play about small-town frustration, she came striding out and said a line in that voice you could already hear the—significance in—some line about 'When is the next bus?' or something like that, and I looked at her, and I heard the voice, and I said: Well, she's been handed a hell of a lot, but what do you do with it? Maybe she can't memorize a long part. Maybe she's legally blind and has learned her stage moves by rote. Maybe she's worth thirty-five million dollars and is only doing this once, for a hoot. But if none of those things is true and that girl wants a *career,* well I think I can give it to her."

He smiled. "That was pretty ballsy of me. Hell, *I* didn't have a career. Taught a little acting and directed a couple of little things. Done radio. Talk about chutzpah. I sat there and said to myself: Baby, I'll make you a star. Just like that. And of course the weirdest part of all is that I did."

"Yeah," I murmured, "that you did." I was lying on the long white couch. I didn't lie around other people's living rooms as a rule, even Axie's. "How did you—approach her, anyway?"

"Just went backstage after that performance, found her taking off her makeup next to the furnace and asked her out. We didn't go to Sardi's. Too far uptown, and they wouldn't have given me the time of day. Who the hell was I?

"There was this place called Tony's, and they did know me there, and we sat in the corner booth and had ravioli. And we talked.

"After two glasses of Chianti, I began to get a perspective on things, and said to myself, I don't know if this broad—sorry, that's the way I talked in those days, before

I finished growing up—I have no way of knowing if this broad can act, has any talent, any sensitivity, can enter into a character. She's striking, she's got a voice. So maybe she should go to Radio City Music Hall and become a Rockette. I don't know if there's an *actress* in there!

"There was only one way to find out, so I enrolled her in my little acting class which met in my little apartment. I worked with her and eventually I found out that she *could* act, that with a lot of work she could get past her own personality, and it was—it is a strong one, isn't it? I was able to get her to go past Axie Reed and immerse herself in a character in a play, *provided* that that character was not too different from herself. If there was a bridge she could cross from herself to that character, then, with a lot of work—Axie could sink into that character and give one hell of a performance.

"You remember that period in the theater? Around 1950? Stanislavsky was God Almighty then, or at least the way Stanislavsky was understood in New York. And Lee Strasberg was his high priest, and the holy of holies was the Actors Studio. Marlon Brando. Geraldine Page. On and on. Big. Huge. Paradise for a young actor starting out.

"Well, Strasberg caught Axie in a little showcase thing I did with her and he let it be known that he would *allow her into the Actors Studio!* Wow. Heaven. All actors in New York would kill for this. No audition even, just walk in the front door, Miss Reed. We'll put you in a project with Marlon. The greatest opportunity since the Red Sea parted for Moses.

"Do you know what happened?"

"No. Axie never told me about this."

"She turned him down, quietly, politely, and oh-so-

definitely. No, thank you very much, thank you very very
much, no, thank you. Speaking in imagistic terms, I was
staring at her, gaping at her with my mouth hanging open
like an idiot's. See, I'd been working so closely with her,
but I didn't really know her.

"The woman is loyal. She never had to think twice.
She was with me, I was working with her. Go to someone
else, just because he's the most prestigious and influential
acting teacher America has ever seen? Of course not. So,
that was settled. Now. Shall we go to Tony's for ravioli?"

19

There was another guest room on the second floor, and as
the rays of the sun lengthened on the west side of the house
and Doug began to say that maybe he ought to be heading
back—he was saying these lines, but with no conviction—
I invited him to stay over the night. Maybe she would
make a turn back toward life during it. In any case,
it didn't seem fitting to let him go away after only a
few hours in Axie's house, never seeing her. He accepted
quietly.

Pauline came in around five o'clock, and then the three
of us more or less tacitly agreed that a nap was what our
spirits needed, mine fading with the sunshine. I asked Edna
to prepare a dinner for us at eight—that was a good theatrical hour, Dinner at Eight—and I made my way up the
stairs and past Axie's room, where the door was now

always left open, as though that inviting entry could somehow help entice her back, back into this intimate room where even the draperies tried to breathe for her.

In my room, I threw off most of my clothes and lay down on the high old bed. Silence reigned over the house.

Here at Portals, we had somehow not entirely believed in her career as a star. That part of her functioned out of her apartment in New York City. The part of her professional life we saw here was usually that her face would be buried in a script; we saw her reading, thinking.

But I did see her open, the opening night in New York of Axie in her first important movie role. She was twenty-six years old, and I was eighteen, a freshman at the University of Pennsylvania.

It had been at the Sutton Theater in Manhattan, and the name of the movie was *The Provincetown Story,* starring this actress nobody had much heard of, Alexandra Reed, and directed by and written by this guy nobody had much heard of either, Douglas Shore.

It wasn't one of those big showy Hollywood-style premieres with searchlights scraping the sky, of course, it was simply a screening for an invited audience the evening before the movie opened for the public.

We were all in our seats by 4:45 in the afternoon, and there was a certain expectancy in the air: a lot of money had been spent on this picture, a major studio was producing and distributing it, and the fact of an unknown author-director and an unknown actress in the lead aroused a lot of curiosity, at least. There were influential people in the audience, waiting.

Then Axie made her entrance, on the arm of Douglas Shore, swathed in a huge mink coat with blond hair over the collar, striding down the aisle to their seats in the fourth row. At her seat, she turned and swept the theater with that wide smile, and she was sending out something, I didn't know what it was, star quality, warmth, magnetism, something. In any case that blasé New York audience began to applaud, and they really gave her a big reception. They had not yet seen the movie. Most of them had never seen her in anything at all as yet.

But she made them applaud, respond to her, *like* her, when all she had so far done was walk down the aisle of the theater, turn, and smile. She was shaking in her shoes, she told me later, at a pitch of nervousness, not far from panic. What we saw were confidence and warmth and magnetism.

Then the movie began, in "glorious Technicolor," filmed on Cape Cod. Axie played a young woman who ran a saloon there where a lot of local characters hung out. One of the fishermen was in love with her, but he was a drinker and wild and their relationship was stormy. And then there was a real storm, at sea, a ship in distress . . . it was a little old-fashioned even then, a little vintage. But there was a verve to the movie, and after the first fifteen minutes I, at least, could feel the audience warming to it, sinking into it. Basically it was not a drama but a comedy, and among other things Alexandra Reed had to sing a song. Axie, sing? She refused to have the singing dubbed, and what emerged was a kind of contralto, or a torch singer, a sound not unlike Marlene Dietrich's, husky and sensuous and conveying feeling, not entirely vocalizing.

But what struck me most as this movie proceeded were the facets of Axie that the camera discovered, things I had barely glimpsed that the camera carefully explored. They lighted her face to bring out its shape, its contours, and the camera came close up onto her great eyes and seemed to reveal her spirit, her secret self, a certain idealism which I had only vaguely glimpsed, but in this movie I saw, clearly.

The last shot was of a fishing smack proceeding at twilight slowly out to sea, the music rose, THE END, and the audience began to applaud in earnest, and the house-lights came up and Axie was flashing that encompassing smile, and I knew that she was going to be a star and to move far out of my orbit, and yet I was very happy and I cried.

FOUR

20

That night, Sunday night, Axie drifted further from us than ever.

She was no longer on a riverboat going up the Nile, nor was she on the Talouris yacht, the *Pacificus*. Her awareness that she was in the intensive care unit at Southampton Hospital disappeared, together with any linkage to the party or to Portals.

She was in a tent, and she was in the desert, any desert. She was lying prone, tied down, and the only sign of life was through an aperture in this tent where she could see some dim and rather distant light and hear the murmur of voices.

The one fact she could remember was the button beside her tied left hand. She pressed it. A woman in white came in and said something in English. Axie could not speak because tubes went through her mouth and down her throat but she felt she could convey her urgent wish nevertheless: Take me with you, she cried desperately, voicelessly, take me toward that light, let me join you and your companions around that light; I heard some laughing just a minute ago, a low, warm laugh; how I need to be near that, near someone laughing in that low, warm way; take me over to that light and that low laughter so that I can go on, because left alone here, strapped down and so confused and so *weak,* I need that light and that laughter and you and your companions around me if I am to go on.

She had always gathered people around her; anywhere she went there had been audiences, thousands of people had gathered to watch her and laugh at her jokes and applaud her songs and she had worked hard for thirty years to hold them; and now, now that she needed just three or four, just a little band, a tiny group, those people by that distant light, she couldn't have them, she must stay here alone—for the woman in white who had spoken English to her was disappearing back through that aperture in the tent and back toward that light and to rejoin her companions, and Alexandra must remain alone here, so confused, terribly alone, all she had ever worked for swept away, and herself left stranded and helpless in this tent, in the desert somewhere.

Time drifted on, there was daylight around her and then a man in white came in: she had seen him before; a compact gray-haired man in white. "I'm your doctor, Miss Reed, and you must just continue to lie there and rest. Your cousin has been here and other close friends. They will come to see you as soon as you are a little better. We have just had a phone call and he asked us to tell you that it was Doug, that he's staying in your house in Water Mill, and that he is always there any time you need him."

The doctor quietly checked here and there, and Axie thought: Yes, I have seen you, here in this tent—no. No. This is not a tent at all, this is intensive care and this is Southampton Hospital and I was at that party at the museum and yes, that message was from Doug and he is thank God staying at Portals, Nick has God bless him invited Doug to stay there and I have *people* out there who love me and always have and whom I love and I have *got* to cling to these realities and not drift back again into last night's sick delusions and that awful *longing* I felt for that distant light and the little band of chuckling people around it.

I know where I am again and I will not let myself lose that realization. I will not. There is no tent and there is no desert and most of all I am *not* alone and abandoned.

Douglas Shore is here, just a couple of miles away, in my house in Water Mill. He hasn't been there very often; funny, the way I always kept my life compartmentalized, as though I was protecting something, protecting my career and my talent from the trivialities of Southampton with all its parties, and protecting Southampton from the tough, blunt, hard-working and no-nonsense world of the New York theater. As for letting Southampton and the movie world collide: never. Only Keith Miller bridged both, and he was exceptional. Keith Miller. "Get Out of Town." What a good dancer. We are turning so smoothly around the dance floor on that raised platform and I can feel many eyes on us, well, on me, and I can feel that they are admiring—I have always been able to feel that when it is there—and we are turning so gracefully, so smoothly, how nice that he is a good three inches taller than I am, even in my heels, and we are turning smoothly and—

. . . rolling along equally smoothly but in a vehicle, I am lying down, strapped down, a siren very nearby and two young men in white: an ambulance.

Did someone shoot me?

Douglas Shore. I will not give up Douglas even though I have decided—I had decided to give up acting. He still gives classes in acting when possible in New York. I know: I can work with him there. I have thirty years of experience, I mean in front of a camera and in front of an audience. There I have the experience and he has not.

Oh, she sighed inwardly and deeply, what a wonderful thought.

Yes, love, yes well Douglas, yes I did love him. I was attracted to him the first time I saw him, in that cellar in the Village. That's why I accepted his invitation, kind of a curt one, to have supper in some Italian place. Yes, I accepted not because I thought he knew the first thing about acting or could possibly have any influence on what I was trying to do but because I thought he was interesting and attractive, and had blue eyes which I found in the candlelight in that little Italian place were much bluer than I had first noticed, rather large and very blue and . . . sincere. A theater guy, I learned, an aspirant in the tough New York theater but all the same, sincere. And blue eyes.

And then working with him and seeing his humanity and his treatment, not just of me, but of his other students, a rather wan girl and an unbelievably intense young man and some others, the way he drew them out without injuring them, well, I fell in love with that too and he made me know that he wanted to come closer to me even than this most intimate work, and that meant of course a sexual relationship and I had not—quite—had a sexual relationship, there was the time stepping over the low stone wall when Spyro had gripped my hand and I had not stumbled and there had been several other brushes with complete sexual commitment too, a number of such near misses and last-minute backing-offs and was I becoming a sexual tease I asked myself in trepidation and the beginnings of self-loathing, and now there was this man at the center of my life, my work, Douglas Shore, and that was what he wanted from me and the wonderful part was that I had no doubts at all, this time; this was right, this was the coming together of the desire and the man, and strangely enough the only issue left to be decided was *where*.

Your place or mine? Ugh. A certain cheapness threatened to invade our relationship around the edges, a creeping decay stole toward us, and to me the reason for that was New York City! A young director and his favorite little aspiring actress hopping into bed together either in his pad in the Village or her walk-up on Third Avenue: my entering a sexual relationship for the first time in my life was threatened with turning into a shopworn cliché, just one more trashy little New York shack-up.

Well, I wouldn't have it. And that left Douglas Shore puzzled, for I had fully responded when he had taken me into his arms after the others had left following a class, and I suppose I sent out little messages, glances or tones of voice or something, which told anyone as sensitive and observant as Doug that yes, I was willing, and yes, it was going to happen.

So why did I break off, why did I go home, why did I say good night on the sidewalk in front of my little building instead of asking him to come up?

The specter of Alexandra Reed as The Tease rose threateningly up before both of us. Was that what he was beginning to think of me? Of course it was. What else could he be thinking, what else was my behavior allowing him to think?

Something had to be done, now.

I thought of Portals, of course. But it was dead of winter, February; the pipes in Portals had been drained, and even though it might be romantic to warm ourselves solely at the fireplaces, lacking central heating, not being able to wash a face nor flush a toilet was not really conducive to the dream of passion.

And then into my mind drifted the state of Vermont. Up in the far hills there, beyond the old homestead a family connection still inhabited in Bennington, up toward the mountains there was a tiny village, a hamlet, called Attenborough Bridge. There was and still is a long, worn, gray and beautiful covered bridge spanning a rocky, tumbling stream there. And there is an inn, a white, narrow Greek Revival four-storied pillared manse I had driven by so many times but never entered. That was where, I ruled to myself, Douglas Shore and I would shatter the last barriers and find what we would find.

Something traditional lurked in this choice; I would go back to the highlands of my fathers and go on to this new stage of life there. I felt it was right then; I understand why it was right now. I was seeking to reconcile my family and my background and my past with a sexual affair with a New York theater man: I had no doubts about the man, but it was the symbolism that drove me on. I must meld these two sides of my life together; I could *not* join myself with him in some room in the city; up there in the mountains, in that white sort of Greek temple, the Attenborough

Bridge Inn, there I would fuse the different parts of my life into a whole.

We got there at dusk: blueness spreading over the surrounding immaculate snowfields, a fire contentedly snapping and hissing in the grate, thick rugs and old furniture and a murmurous dining room with decorative glass on shelves, and copious helpings of pot roast. Wine? Well, let me have a look down cellar: maybe we still got some of that batch left. And they did have, a Pommard; it was past its prime but still drinkable, very drinkable and strong. They were beginning to look a little dubiously at us and perhaps wondering if we had lied in registering as man and wife—after all, this was 1952—but we were past caring whether they believed that or not.

In the room there was one high four-poster bed and there appeared to be someone already asleep in it when we went up after the dinner and the wine. Specifically, there seemed to be an extremely pregnant woman asleep beneath the white feather comforter, enormously pregnant, impossibly pregnant. Then, pulling back the comforter, we saw revealed a curving wooden frame holding a pot of coals suspended between the sheets, to warm them.

And they were warm, the sheets, and we did not need their warmth for he gave me his and more and then more, and I returned to him a heat I had not known was inside me and we broke through and pierced that barrier and went on into the thrilled completion behind it.

I was his; I loved him; he loved me and was in love with me and now our relationship was everything it could be. By the following morning in the Attenborough Bridge Inn we were as far into our relationship as we could ever go, as close, and as mutually joined as could ever be.

Because I could go no further.

I could not go further, I couldn't, I couldn't.

Wine, that bottle of Pommard, how rich it was, rich red vintage wine and its marvelous moisture and here and now I am so dry and so thirsty and my mouth and throat are like the desert and please God if I could have a glass of water, no I cannot ask for that, what a privilege, a glass of water, just a half—a quarter of a glass of water. Why is there no water?

This overpowering thirst, this intolerable dryness had been with Axie for a long time but now, as her mind was clearing, the discomfort of it, the intolerableness came in force to the surface.

I will never take drinking a long, cold, pure glass of water for granted again in my life. What a privilege, what joy.

I am tied to this bed, I am not getting repeat *I am not getting* enough air and I am expiring of thirst. Of course my whole body aches too and I am terribly swollen along my right side and must look like some purple monster when they lift the sheet, but all of these other problems I can tolerate if only God would allow me to have just a little water.

Why did I ever drink soda pop or tea or beer or wine, let alone anything as raw and as awful as liquor when I could, at any time at all, have taken a long, cold, pure glass of water!

I will never make that mistake again in the future. That is, well, if there, well, if there is, well, if . . . well . . .

The nurse came in, a different one from the woman in white in the desert with her chuckling friends. This nurse was plump and brisk and preoccupied.

Axie agitated her left hand as much as she could in its

confinement. The nurse finally noticed. Axie pantomimed writing. It took some time before this nurse came to understand the mime. You klutz, Axie snarled inwardly. *Everybody* understands and has always understood my miming immediately.

She tried to consume her rising anger. The plump nurse ambled out, presumably in search of pad and pencil, but Axie could see the ones she had used before on the little table by the wall.

She tried to smother her anger. Finally the nurse returned and put the pad where she could write on it and gave her the pencil.

For the next couple of minutes Axie, tubes in her throat, tied down, struggled to convey to this nurse that she could not write unless her left wrist was released. Some time passed before the nurse comprehended this, and more time before the nurse was able to resolve the issues in her mind and finally untie the wrist.

On the pad Axie scrawled in her terrible, crazed block letters: I NEED SOME WATER.

"Oh no, you can't have water," the nurse said in an unarguable tone.

Desperately Axie underlined the words, then looked up agonizingly, pleadingly, meltingly, she hoped, at this adamant woman.

Then Axie scrawled: ASK THE DOCTOR.

"Those are doctor's orders," the nurse said.

Axie underlined the words again and again: *ASK THE DOCTOR.*

Now on her face Axie tried to express authority, even a kind of threat.

The nurse glanced over her visage, busied herself for half a minute, and then left the room.

After a while she returned with the compact gray-haired man in the white coat.

Giving him the melting, suffering, last-extremity open-eyed gaze which had knocked them dead at the climax of *Again the River,* Axie underlined *I NEED SOME WATER* once again.

"Miss Reed," said the doctor in a very reasonable voice, "your system is getting the water it needs through the intravenous feeding going into your shoulder. I know that your mouth and throat are very parched. I hope you understand that your *system* is getting the water it needs." He paused and looked down at her. She looked with her great eyes into his: Do something more, she conveyed with all the suffering humanity she could pour into that gaze.

"Nurse," he finally said, "you can give her a few bits of shaved ice. Miss Reed, the little bits of ice will help. We cannot give you much. It could be disturbing to your stomach. You could vomit. With the tubing, well—you must *not* vomit, we cannot risk upsetting your stomach in any way. I understand the discomfort you are going through—" *You cannot possibly understand it, have any grasp of it at all, unless you have gone through it yourself,* she rasped inwardly— "and we can just give you little—tiny bits of shaved ice for a while, to help relieve the discomfort." Then he left.

The nurse was holding a little plastic cup and she dipped the tip of a straw in it and then placed this tip, with its tiny mound of ice, on Axie's tongue, and as the ice melted into water there and flowed through her dryness-ravaged mouth and on down her Sahara throat Axie experienced a dream of communion; this was a communion, not in church but in life, a communion of her body with the most fundamental gift of nature. Water. She gazed at the nurse; I love you totally, Axie thought, for your hand and that little straw in it and that mound of ice you just gave me. If I gaze at you with all the fullness of my love perhaps you will give me a second mound. Whether for that reason or not, after hesitating, this marvel of a woman, Florence Nightingale's spiritual heiress, conveyed to her tongue a second tiny mound, and this too melted and flowed magically down through her mouth and throat. "We must not upset your stomach," the nurse then murmured, and moved away, but it had been enough, for this moment at least, water still existed and tiny amounts of it, at least, could be given to her safely. There was hope.

21

The Talouris family arrived at Portals unannounced around seven o'clock that evening. Still upstairs in my room, I heard the engine of an automobile come down the gravel driveway, around the water tower and into the circle of gravel next to the East Porch. I am one of those people who can classify cars by the sound of their engines, and this was a very expensive car. I looked down at it from my window: out of a stretch deep blue Mercedes-Benz stepped a tall, ample blond woman, Norma Talouris, who was Spyro's mother, then his father, rather short and big-shouldered, in a white suit, then Spyro's brother, Lambros, Axie's former husband, in a dark suit, and finally Spyro, in blue slacks and a white polo shirt, in other words, not dressing like the other members of his family for this taut occasion. Spyro assuredly marched to a different drummer. His wife Janie was not with them, Spyro being one of those husbands who acquired a wife like a chest of drawers, useful at home and to be left there.

I could hear them on the porch and then coming into the entrance hall; they did not knock on the door at Portals, of course. I went along the upstairs hall in the blue bathrobe to the banister overlooking the entrance hall and, looking down as they hesitated there, said: "I'll be right down. Axie's director is here, you remember, Douglas Shore. We'll both be right down." Fortunately, Pauline Marsh had gone out somewhere.

Mr. Talouris—Stamos—scowled wordlessly up at me. He didn't disapprove of me, I knew that, knew that in his mind I fell into that large category classified as "harmless." So his scowl probably referred to Douglas Shore.

I stuck my head into the room where Douglas was lying on the bed, reading a script. "The Talourises are here, Spyro and his brother and parents." Douglas rolled his eyes at me. "It won't be so bad. After all, tonight we've all got one thing in common, haven't we."

Ten minutes later we were arranged around the living room, rather wanly illuminated by the evening sun, no fire in the big fireplace in August, Axie's portrait semi-obscured in shadow, shadows in the corners of the big room, a kind of strained silence hanging over it.

The Talourises were one of those families that seem to have a certain youthfulness built into the genes: none of them, including the Talouris-by-marriage Norma, was aging as most people did. Stamos, who must be now around eighty, appeared to be an energetic sixty-year-old. Norma, perhaps seventy, seemed more like fifty-five, and neither

Spyro nor Lambros really appeared to be thoroughly middle-aged men; both were lean and athletic-looking and with a definite youthful air still clinging to them.

"What can I do to help?" asked Norma Talouris in her melodious, low-pitched voice. Blond and creamy and almost queenly in a relaxed way, she was wearing a lavender chiffon dress and a wide-brimmed straw garden hat. Norma, as the cant expression of the time would have it, did her own thing. She wore her own style of clothes. Stamos would have utterly crushed her long before, had she been otherwise. She was Spyro's mother; Lambros was the son of an earlier marriage, to a Greek woman. He was tall and a little cadaverous and dark; Spyro medium-height and tight-knit and ruddy.

"You've just hit on our big frustration," I answered her. "There's practically nothing any of us can do."

"I talked to Dr. LaBrianca twice, yesterday and today," Stamos cut through. "I am in touch with the best lung man in New York. A helicopter could get her there in half an hour. LaBrianca talked me out of that. Fear of coma. No shock of any kind needed now, not even a flight in a helicopter."

"We'll get her any specialist she might need," Lambros murmured concurringly.

"She doesn't need a specialist," murmured Spyro in an almost surly tone.

"What does she need?" inquired Lambros.

After a silence Spyro muttered, "A miracle." He was slouched in an armchair, legs stretching in front of him. "I have a holy medal . . . well . . . a little coin I found on Samos . . ."

"In the Hippocrates Grove, wasn't it?" murmured Norma.

"Yeah." He let out a breath. "Good as anything else, if you ask me." He was silent again. "Maybe better."

"Did she know what it was?" asked Douglas in a subdued version of his actor's voice across the room.

Spyro rather slowly raised his eyes. "Yeah." Then something came into his mind; he turned to me. "Where's that goddam lady photographer?"

"Out photographing, I guess. She's not in her room."

"Why don't you kick her ass out of here?"

I looked at him for a little. Axie invited her here? It's not my house? I rejected both: those answers wouldn't sit well with Spyro, and anyway they weren't the ultimate reason. "She's a journalist," I said quietly. "The photograph of Axie . . . of Axie . . . lying on . . . well, that photograph was bad enough—"

"The worst," growled Lambros. "I wanted to kill whoever took it." Looking at him for a second or two, I reflected: I wouldn't want you to want to kill *me*. Spyro is all surface hostility and abrasiveness. Looking at Lambros I surmised: you're subdued and contained and controlled. But I think you're the one with the true family ruthlessness, inherited from your father; and it's interesting that you're the one against all odds that Axie chose to marry, bypassing Spyro here. I would not want you to want to kill me. As for Stamos, of course, if *he* wanted to kill me I think he'd go ahead and do it, successfully covering up the crime afterward.

"She needs to want to get well," put in Norma quietly.

"Yes," I muttered. "That's what the doctor says."

"You don't have to be a doctor to understand that," she went on in her calming voice. "She is—how old?"

"Fifty," said Lambros.

"Yes," sighed Norma, "well, yes. Past most of her

life, through the crucial years. And what does she make of them, lying in the intensive care unit? I don't care how . . . how withdrawn from—us she may be now, she'll be able to consider what's past in her life. Will it be enough? Based on the past, is there reason to go on, drive herself with every ounce of strength she's got, all the will, the *discipline,* to rise up out of this and live on?"

Two seconds' silence and then from Douglas: "Yes." Quietly and firmly and carryingly.

"You said that like you were voting," said Stamos flatly, leaning out of his chair, big hand on knee, looking challengingly at him, sidelong.

"Did I?" I liked his self-possession; Douglas was not the man to be afraid of the power of money; it wasn't his realm. "I know her."

These words hung in the living room. Metaphorically, the three Talouris men and the one Talouris woman stared at them. The word *know* has several meanings, including the Biblical one. So it hung there in the middle of the room, and it took some time, in the piercing silence, for it to dissolve and dematerialize.

"How about some supper?" I put in, getting up. "Edna's usually prepared for last-minute guests. I'll tell her to set four more places."

They were all silent and then Norma said, "Yes, that would be nice. After all, this is the telephone we want to be near," and she patted it, on the table beside her chair. "If Edna needs anything more, we can send Andrew back to the house for it." Andrew was the chauffeur, by now having a cup of coffee or something more in the kitchen with Edna.

"Where's the dog?" asked Spyro, his mind running to this household.

"Edna must have him in the kitchen."

"I'll go get him," he said, standing up.

Children, animals, these were the creatures Spyro liked and felt comfortable with. He did not with me, not entirely with his own family, God knows not with Douglas, and so he went to fetch the company of a being he could trust.

Half an hour later we were at the long, refectory-style oaken dinner table.

The dining room ran the entire width of the house, thirty-eight feet, from bow window with ferns at the east end to French doors and roses at the west.

Here Axie had presided so interestingly, so gaily, so incisively at the head of the table for many a long dinner hour and two hours and three hours, red wine in decanters being passed around, cigarette and cigar smoke—she did not smoke herself but did not object to, didn't seem to notice, others who smoked at her table.

None of us, not even Stamos, took her high-backed armchair at the head of the long table. As the roast lamb and roast potatoes were being passed I could so easily visualize Axie leaning out of that chair toward us, her penetrating voice cutting through our murmured remarks: "Oh stop being so morbid, all of you. Either I'll make it or I won't make it. I've *lived*. Don't make me some *gloomy* person in your lives. I've never been gloomy. Anybody here seen any good movies?"

That voice again: it now and then invaded me. I looked across the table at Doug. "Have you seen the latest James Bond movie? I have a better title for it: *Violent Twaddle*."

He looked up at me, a little unprepared for my question, and then approving of it, probably understanding why I had asked it.

On either side of him Stamos and Lambros stopped

what they were saying—medical matters—to Spyro and Norma, on either side of me. All four stopped and looked puzzled (Norma), opaque (Lambros), impatient (Stamos) and disgusted (Spyro).

"Yes," answered Douglas easily, "saw it just last week, in a big theater in Manhattan, with five other people coming in out of the heat wave."

"Haven't you got anything better to talk about than movies?" cut in Spyro.

"Have you seen it?" Douglas inquired politely and infuriatingly of him.

Spyro of course ignored the question. Over his shoulder to me he shot, "Don't let your money limitations interfere in any way with Axie's treatment, that's what Dad and I have been discussing just now. While you were at the movies."

I settled back in my chair: "There's a family trust going back, oh, eighty, a hundred years, for just such situations. The Reed Family Trust. In Boston. They will handle everything, financially speaking."

That stopped him. It wasn't true, but I was not going to take this new-rich arrogance from Spyro, who had himself earned none of it. I would if necessary hold up banks to see that every nickel needed for Axie's care was available.

"Oh," sighed Norma on my right, "old families. They did so prepare for the future, didn't they?" Spyro resumed eating busily.

He was and always had been one of those few people in my life the mere sight of whom made me taut with edgy aggressiveness.

Stamos, as usual, appeared to have been paying no attention to what we others were saying: he heard every word always, but seemed never to do so. Now he said,

"I think there's nothing more we can do for her in terms of treatment. I've talked to the best people in New York, *they've* talked to Dr. LaBrianca and then gotten back to me, and this information tells me that everything that can be done is being done. Yes, it all boils down to that she's got to want to get well. She will fight, of course she will. So, what's left is controlling the publicity, the public impression, her image. Where is this woman, the one with the camera?"

"I guess she'll turn up eventually," I said. "She's still ensconced here. I think it's better that way, to answer your question of an hour ago, Spyro. I've got her under close surveillance here. I can control what information she gets, to a certain extent."

"Her image," echoed Douglas to himself drily, perhaps a little bitterly.

Once again, as with his "I know her," his words drove the Talourises into a disturbed, frustrated—in Spyro's case seething—silence.

"It's important," Lambros finally said flatly.

"Oh yes . . . yes," murmured Douglas, his mind apparently elsewhere.

"She has always valued her career so, hasn't she," put in Norma placatingly. "Well, Mr. Shore, you would know all about that, wouldn't you."

"Yes." He looked across at her with interest, and respect. "Axie was devoted to her work. Not the same thing as caring so much about your 'image' though, is it." Everybody was phrasing their statements in the form of questions, but not being interrogative. "She wanted to get it right, in all her roles. Nothing was ever too much trouble for that. Then when it came to the press, well Axie just said to them and did in front of them, if they happened to be around, exactly what she wanted to say and do. She never shaped anything according to how it would look in print. They all loved her, the reporters, because she was such good copy. They protected her a lot, just arbitrarily cut out things she would say that could really damage her. Like the time she told some reporter during lunch at the Brown Derby that Hollywood wasn't just tinsel, it was old tinsel, that the heads of all the major studios were little boys playing musical chairs, and that when it came to money they made drug dealers look like philanthropists. She also said they knew about as much about dramatic art as Hitler knew about racial equality. Provocative, you know. *Good copy.* I was going to speak to the guy interviewing her, try to stop it. But toward the end of the interview, when Axie happened to be looking the other way, he just winked at me, and that was all. The next day his paper printed a good interview of her, lively, but he saved her, leaving the parts out that could be really destructive." Douglas wiped his mouth with his napkin. "That's the kind of protection she inspired in the media. Of course, when she gave interviews on television, live, that is when I sweated blood. Managed to keep her off most of those shows, most of the time. So much for her 'image.' Her 'image' with the public was and is just Axie, being herself. Right now she's fighting for her life—"

"If she *is* fighting," muttered Spyro, speaker of unpleasant truths and possibilities, to himself.

"—and I think the public ought to know it," Douglas finished. "They will anyway. You can't keep these reporters from finding things like that out. All those nurses, those orderlies, even if the doctors keep quiet."

"Her image doesn't mean shit," muttered Spyro.

Stamos glared at him, a little bit of incredulousness

around the edges of that glare. A direct contradiction of Stamos by either of his sons, any of his relatives, any of the people he worked with, was an occurrence as rare as a cloud in the summer Aegean. Everything stopped on their island, Paxos, when a long cloud would pass over on some summer's day, wandering from Libya vaguely off toward Russia, a drifter, lost. So also was such a blunt contradiction of Stamos Talouris in his presence. He continued to glare at Spyro, who was looking down into his lap. "What do you think we should do?" he then demanded of him.

Spyro looked up. Then he said one word: "Pray."

Nobody knew how to comment. Spyro simply did not think as other people did, and so was often disconcertingly at odds with all others around him, and with their impression of what he himself was like. "I gave her a medal . . ." and "If she will fight . . ." he had said, and now, from Spyro, whom neither Norma nor Janie could virtually ever lure to church, "Pray."

"Well," said Lambros drily, perhaps a little sarcastically, "I think we're all going to have to think along lines a little more practical than *that*."

From his head-down posture Spyro looked up and across at his brother. It was a mean look.

There was something peculiar and even unprecedented coming into the relationships of this family. Because of Axie I had spent time with the Talourises ever since I was a little boy, and the one attitude which had always prevailed anywhere and everywhere was their monolithic unity. They did not fight among themselves, they did not bicker or criticize or, so it seemed to me, even occasionally frown at one another. They agreed. They were united against the world. They were a Greek family, not socially accepted in the United States, not entirely, not in the beginning in any case. Very well, they would live content among themselves, with the visiting relatives from Greece and the business associates here and the sports figures and the movie people who were only too eager to accept their friendship and their hospitality and their yacht and their Greek island. In this setting would the Talourises live and flourish and be happy. As far as I could see, they had succeeded in doing so; Stamos and Norma got along with each other and the next generation and now the rising generation below that; Spyro and Janie appeared congenial and content in the Spyro-dominated pattern of their lives; Lambros, it's true, had been divorced from Axie, but most amicably, and he had remarried, and there were three children by that union, and his wife, too, Elena, was Greek and seemed willing to efface herself and fit easily into the family pattern. And so they remained, it appeared, content and secure, and always, instinctively, united and self-supporting and never contentious among themselves.

But here at the long oaken dinner table of Portals, I was for the first time detecting fissures, tensions rising to the surface, intolerances of one another showing through.

The pressure of Axie's ordeal was in some way shaking their monolithic edifice to its always-solid-seeming foundation. There had been more than one family crisis in the past, and yet their unquestioning family loyalty and mutual support had survived unscathed, unthreatened. But this ordeal that Axie was passing through, this dance of death going on in the intensive care unit of Southampton Hospital, seemed to have shaken loose some cracks in the solid façade at last. Perhaps it was simply because they could do nothing, as I could not. They were not used to that. Stamos had always been able to do something, and usually something effective, about anything. Spyro and Lambros had not been far behind, and Norma had benefited by having the hurdles in front of her cleared away by her men.

Now they could only sit and talk.

And there was guilt here, too. The tacit understanding within the family and outside it was that the marriage of Axie to Lambros had broken up because he attempted to treat her the way a Greek man treats a Greek wife, and Axie could simply not endure it. She was an American, she was an artist, and she was a celebrity, and she could not be kept, metaphorically, at home in the kitchen. Lambros had not tried to do so, I knew that, but at this moment they wanted to blame someone, and he was the obvious choice.

The family had failed her. Beneath everything, they were all aware of Axie's idealism, and her marrying Lambros had been based on that. "Until death do us part." She had meant every syllable. And his casual playboy freewheeling man-of-the-world international-tycoon behavior had finally forced her to break this vow, they thought. They in their Greekness had failed her, undermined her dedication to a lifelong marriage, and forced her out of the family.

And now she was at death's door.

They simmered at each other. Who was responsible, Lambros for the way he had treated her or Stamos for teaching him to relegate wives to the background? Why hadn't Lambros had the intelligence to recognize a different kind of woman and treat her accordingly? Why had Lambros thrust himself into Axie's life at all, and not left her alone in her great friendship with Spyro, where she would

always have been safe? And hadn't Spyro really, ulti-
mately, believed that he and Axie would marry, and only
finally settled for Janie after his older brother had taken
her?

Axie and her peculiar position in this family and their
special emotions toward her had truly shaken it at last.
Suspicious and resentful, they sat at the table, doubtless
resenting me and despising Douglas Shore. This was a
Talouris family drama, but they were not to be permitted
to act it out among themselves, and the reason for that
was that Axie's orbit extended far beyond them, including
not just Douglas and me in its inner circle, but in an outer
ring all those uncounted loyal people who walked up to
box offices and bought tickets to her movies and plays,
who only had to see her photograph on the cover of a
magazine to buy the magazine. Those uncounted people
in America and in other countries too had their rights; Axie
had reached out and touched them, and so they had their
rights, and so did their representatives, the working press,
the media, Pauline Marsh.

We were back in the living room sipping brandy when
she joined us. She came swinging into the room, and even
the way she entered, the way she swung with a loose,
confident American stride into the living room offended,
I could sense, the Europeanness in the Talourises. Don't
walk in as though you owned the place, I could feel them
muttering inwardly; be a woman, and slip in quietly,
gracefully.

In white slacks and a loose blue shirt she moved briskly
from one to the other of them as I introduced her: none
of the men budged. If you were a lady and knew how to
behave, they telegraphed, we would stand up; since you're

clearly an American woman off the streets, we won't bother to stand. Of the family, only Norma greeted her with any cordiality; and only Douglas stood up.

None of this appeared to make any impression on Pauline. She flung herself into a deep armchair, the nape of her neck resting at the top of the chair's back, her pelvis sprung forward, legs outstretched. With this posture I saw that she was now losing Norma, too: now they all found her intolerable, but then they would have anyway: the photograph of Axie, lying unconscious on the grass, shot from above, had been more than enough. Maybe Pauline knew this, and perhaps her breezy, impudent entrance had been deliberate and defiant. "Screw you," as they said in the newsroom of the *Washington Star*, may have been her mood, and to offend these people her goal; if so, she had brilliantly reached it.

". . . so Janie and the kids will be out for the weekend," Spyro went on, "but there's still plenty of room in the house of course, and maybe you and Mother'll stay on for the weekend." Spyro now owned the rambling Talouris house on the beach, which Stamos and Norma had built. "And you'll stay on too, right?" he said, turning to Lambros.

"I don't think any of us wants to leave," he muttered. And they went on into details of whether Elena was coming with her children, and rooms and cars and the family plane, and if they had got onto the subject of the weekly laundry list I wouldn't have been surprised. Any subject would do as long as it excluded and if possible insulted Pauline. She didn't exist in the room. Norma did not enter entirely into this, and I noticed her darting a glance once or twice in Pauline's direction.

Then Pauline's sharp voice cut into the room: "I'd

offer you my room here, in case you need it, but Axie specifically invited me for as long as I cared to stay. And nobody would like to go against what Axie wanted now, would they." There was another of them: a question which wasn't a question. She looked with deliberation from one to the other of the Talourises.

Stamos stared at her even more fixedly than the others, and then he got swiftly up. Oh Jesus, what now? I groaned inwardly. Short and compact, he strode toward her and then his wide mouth broke into a grin. "Come over here, miss," he said in his rumbling voice, solicitously taking her hand, "over with me to that settee over there. We want to talk. Come." Pauline gazed up at him ponderingly for a couple of seconds, and then slowly rose out of the chair. He took her arm companionably; and escorted her to the far corner of the room, past the grand piano, to where there was a small white settee between two ficus trees. He seated her almost gallantly, and then settled in beside her. In a stage move, he turned back toward us. All the world's a stage, I reflected as my nerves began to relax, and all the men and women are actors right out of the Actors Studio, or else classes with Douglas Shore. Stamos, I was noticing, was an accomplished performer when he wanted to be. "Go on with your talk, family business," he said. "This lady here and I are going to get acquainted."

When she came in, he had started to treat her with contempt, but now Stamos was making a quick turnabout. He had thought better of it, and he had thought better of it fast. He turned to her and began conversing in a low, warm tone of voice, and Norma, who clearly knew her cues in Stamos's playlets, said in her pleasing tone, raising it perhaps a little: "I think when Axie is better, when the crisis is over, and she is convalescing, I think then we will take her to Paxos. Can you think of anywhere better for her, after what she is having to go through?"

Spyro and Lambros were silent, beginning to stare now with thoughtful eyes fixed on a far-off place, and I could enter into their minds' pictures, too, for I had visited Paxos, and more than once, and on two occasions for months at a time, had even been for a week the only person besides servants at the Talouris place there and had had to give all the orders: What shall you have for lunch, Mr. Nick? Do you want the boat—that was the *Pacificus,* many hundreds of tons of "boat"—this afternoon? I had once been the lord of that Aegean kingdom for one entire week, and I knew its sun which seemed to give life, and its moon which turned white-washed lanes into phosphorescent moonways, and the ever-changing sea, and the winds.

Yes . . . if Axie . . . when Axie was convalescent, we would go . . . I would leave everything, too, and we would go to Paxos.

FIVE

22

She spent the next several days breathing. That was all that mattered, all that she could accomplish, all that there was to concentrate upon. To breathe.

The respirator hanging above her and aimed at her mouth rhythmically pumped air and while there was still not enough air, not enough, nevertheless it was air, and she must breathe it, and she must breathe it the right way, not trying too hard, not gulping but as though breathing naturally. She must not force, and she must not slacken.

It was rather like acting. Timing was everything, that and a naturalness which had to be constructed by experience and will. She had built her characters that way, so that they *seemed* to be behaving naturally, but really it was artifice. Actors who were really themselves onstage or before the camera disgusted her as they lounged self-indulgently through their roles. That was not the way it was meant to be, she knew. Acting was not life: it was artificial, and it was theater, and it should seem like life to the audience. But ordinarily, in life, people did not really move or speak or even sit down the way she and other real actors in a play or movie did. They enlarged and stylized life in their roles, and then passed on this illusion to their audiences. Usually it had worked for her.

And it had to work now too, in breathing, seeming to do it with utmost naturalness, but really concentrating and stylizing and controlling each and every breath, acting as though it were all coming naturally, but really working at it with each intake: not too much, not too hard, just enough, just the right spacing, controlled. She seemed to be making headway.

And what is this all about? she demanded of herself once in a while, as the arduousness of the concentration began to exhaust her frail energies. Just what am I struggling for, straining every nerve for? Life? And what is that going to be in my future, and do I want it and why did they get me to the hospital so fast, wasn't that a theatrically stunning finale there on the grass under the beautiful white silken marquee, surrounded by the cream of Long Island society, in full view of the press?

What an exit.

And she went on with her breathing, giving it all her attention and care. Breathe. She went on with it blindly, devoting every attention to it. Breathe. Why am I doing this, strapped here, career over, failed marriage, not even a lover, no children, why am I straining every nerve and using every wile simply to get the maximum amount of air in just the right way? What's the point of it? Is my future life really going to be so great? Had it ever been, however glittering it may have looked to others? Breathe.

From time to time someone was allowed to come in and stand by her bed and say a few things to her: Lambros, Spyro, and finally Stamos and Norma. Edna too, of course. They all adopted the same manner, calm and quiet and smiling, encouraging. They all came faithfully to make their little contributions to her recovery.

But really it was up to her, and there were times, three o'clock in the morning episodes, when, drained, she asked herself the ultimate: What am I doing? Why am I doing it? Wasn't that my exit, wasn't the play written that way, wasn't I supposed to disappear forever? And what is this coda with its squalor and pain, and why am I living through it? The symmetry has gone out of my life, this is anticlimax. What's ahead of me? Should I really survive this?

The next morning Spyro brought her a color photograph of the little port on Paxos, with its cobbled agora, the few shops and tavernas, the square granite tower of the church and monastery at the center, the fishing caïques tied up at the wharf, all bathed in the clarity of the Greek summer sun. "This is where we're taking you when you're a little better," he whispered. "I'll prop this picture up here on the shelf, so you can look at it whenever you want to. That's where we're going to take you. You'll want Edna and you'll want Bruno, and maybe you'll even want your cousin Nick. Whatever you want."

Axie was only able to manage a kind of smile; she thought of gesturing for pad and pencil to write a grateful word to him, but then she realized it wasn't necessary. Here is this beautiful place in your future, he was saying to her. You will not spend the rest of your life in intensive care, relating singly and solely to a respirator. There are beautiful places out there which you love, and you will see them again.

When he left she let her eyes linger on the picture. Paxos. The turning point of her life had occurred there, and if she had never seen it, she would not have been the actress she became, not have been the woman she was, the woman whom quite a few million people were intermittently fascinated by. Paxos had completed her.

She had not been prepared for it, had not known what to expect there. *The Greek islands* was a phrase like *Paris in the spring* or *a castle in Spain* which had no resonance for her, no meaning. She only knew that it was supposed to be something good. Following her great initial success in *The Provincetown Story* she had been hurried by her studio into three other movies, and she had also had to fulfill two limited-run stage commitments as well. Axie thought she had acquitted herself creditably in all of them, the reviews had been generally favorable and business surprisingly good.

But she was exhausted. That was why her interviews began to be so provocative, too provocative. Comparing the heads of the Hollywood movie studios to Hitler was madness. Fortunately the reporter had, wonder of wonders, censored that remark himself. But she could feel her nerves were becoming overstrained, and her relationship with Douglas, sexual and intense and professional and muddled, was going in circles. And then Spyro, who never allowed himself during even the most intense professional periods of her life to be moved from near the center of it, said to her: "You are coming with Ma and Pa and Lambros and me to our island, and you are going to spend a month there. Is that clear?"

She had looked up at him from her dressing table at the Alvin Theater in New York, where she was about to close in a revival of Lillian Hellman's *The Children's Hour*— she had not been all that good in it, she thought—and after studying his taut, ruddy face for a while she had simply murmured, "All right. Thank you. I'd love to," as though they were talking about a visit to Vermont.

Well, Paxos had assuredly not been anything at all like Vermont, and it had grabbed her and changed her and frightened her.

Every woman must be grabbed and turned inside out and made to face herself starkly and be frightened out of her wits, if she is fully and truly herself, Axie believed. Certainly that had happened to her, there on Paxos, and without it she would simply have been . . . well, an actress, competent, charming she supposed, but with something lacking.

The Talourises had preceded her to the island, and when she had taken the curtain call for *The Children's Hour*, she had changed into traveling clothes and, her baggage ready, the Talouris chauffeur had installed her in a limousine and whisked her to the airport, to the terminal where the family four-engine plane awaited. She had been installed in a sleeping compartment; in the cockpit were two pilots and a navigator; here in the rear there was a steward to look after her; otherwise she was completely alone, being hurtled five thousand miles to an Aegean island. Edna at that time was already her maid but was not yet inseparable from her; the dog of the era, Smokey, was also left behind; Axie was simply bolting headlong toward this strange and remote place, and it was that, together with her nervous fatigue, that probably accounted for the impact made upon her by Greece, by the Aegean, and by

Paxos. She faced them abruptly, and she faced them alone.

Somewhere in the glare of that summer sunlight after she landed, somewhere as the winds whipped over the aft deck of the majestic *Pacificus* bearing her across the sea, beneath that sun and being swept by that wind her importance flew away, the structure she had erected, with Douglas's indispensable aid, of a rising and important young American actress: that young lady in her basic flimsiness fluttered away from her on the wind and was scattered over the tossing sea. What was left was just herself, Alexandra Reed, American woman, a pretty, even striking-looking woman, by no means stupid, rather well-educated. So?

And what did that amount to, she wondered, as she gazed at the ageless and defiant temple of Apollo on the last headland at Sunion; what sort of impression can that make here, she inquired of a white medieval monastery pasted to the side of a cliff.

Tough, gnarled fishermen, wallowing past this ice-white yacht in their shabby caïques, squinted up at her inquisitively, utterly unimpressed; the very crew of the yacht, casually dressed, friendly, similarly seemed to take her for granted. Several of them seemed to be flirting. They appeared not to know or to care whether she was a famous person or a poor relation or a prostitute; it was all somehow the same, under this gorgeously relaxing and implacable sun and this ungovernable wind as it rose and fell. She was a woman, pretty, striking-looking, tall and blond—unusual, in the eyes of these Greeks where the women tended to be small and dark—that was the way the Greeks around her saw her.

No Talouris had met her; all family members were otherwise occupied, and after all, here in Greece, a competent adult woman might be expected to proceed unescorted from a private plane to a private yacht. Coddling was not for Greece. The land was too poor, too stark. Even the richest knew that and acted accordingly. After all, they had not been rich for long. Stamos's family came from Paxos originally, where his father had been a fisherman, and his mother a seamstress. An uncle had gotten into the shipping business and dragged young Stamos in behind him, and from that beginning the fortune had risen. Stamos knew poverty in his bones, and while his wife, Norma, was from a British-Caribbean background, she understood island sparseness very well.

Nobody here was ever going to ask Axie for her autograph, no strange person was going to pop up and take her picture. Nobody gave a damn who she was or had been or thought she was. They saw what they saw, and drew their own raw conclusions.

At the same time that Axie was being stripped of whatever importance she thought she possessed, whatever structured identity had hitherto protected her, she was from the first also being powerfully, irresistibly seduced by this land, this sea, these islands and these people.

As the yacht had pulled out of the port of Piraeus she had stood alone at the railing, wearing a thin pale yellow dress, and gazed at the hills of Attica billowing up behind Athens, so bare, brownish, poignant, stripped of their forests long ago, and now holding little water, barely capable of growing anything useful, these hills, spare and beautiful and tragic, with the sweep of the Athenian metropolis seeming to start just in front of them—centered on the Acropolis, stark and ruined and noble—and then sweep down in a jumble of anonymous and meaningless buildings all the way to Piraeus and the sea. Broken and sun-drenched, the city sprawled beneath these hills and stopped only at the edge of the sea, as though the hodgepodge of glory and poverty which the city embraced would tumble on into the very waves.

Hardly had Axie had time to take in this sweep of classic and tragic before the *Pacificus* was carrying her past the Sunion headland. Standing alone there, slender, defiant, the temple of Apollo seemed to mock her—You say you are a *movie star*? They know you at *Sardi's*?—so thoroughly that to this imagined rebuke she replied inwardly, No I am a student, a student from the New World who has come here to study what you have, all that has been left here by greatness, by the greatest civilization in the history of the world.

The main saloon of the yacht oppressed her, with its grand piano screwed to the floor, its beige wall-to-wall carpeting, the Renoir on the wall, the built-in record player with speakers cunningly concealed here and there: it was the living room of a deluxe Fifth Avenue apartment, and it was here, in the middle of the poverty-stricken Aegean.

She spent almost all of the five-hour trip on deck, watching whatever land they passed, the island with the white monastery pasted to a cliff, and the tough men in the caïques as they took in the look of her.

Paxos was two things at once. On the one hand it was the Talouris house, a long white structure rambling along the edge of a cliff about fifty feet above the sea, a mélange of earlier houses and cottages linked together into this rambling mansion, immaculate white walls inside and out, terraces and balconies, an inner courtyard with two-thousand-year-old amphorae recovered from the floor of the sea, a huge, marble-floored entrance hall—the core building had been a sea-captain's palazzo—and bright-colored furniture and rugs and hangings set against the whiteness of the walls. Beautiful.

On the other hand Paxos itself was simplicity to starkness: there were no motorized vehicles except a few motorcycles: people traveled between the three tiny villages by carriage or donkey. The little restaurants with at most two or three main courses to offer, the tiny tavernas with wine and ouzo and not much else to drink, the old men playing board games, the young men off fishing or trying to make a living somehow, the quick realization that fresh water was a treasure, dragged to the island in a kind of gigantic floating sausage: this collision of worlds seemed possible only in the Aegean. The ultimate truth was very simple: starvation was not far away.

For the first few days she mainly rested and slept. There were few sounds to disturb her: the agonized braying of donkeys as they passed along the cobbled way just the other side of the Talourises' outer wall was the chief one. Sometimes the whining, dirgelike music from a radio at the kitchen end of the house would drift through to her in her dreams and unsettle her vaguely. Who were these people, the Greeks, who responded to such doleful music?

Finally, on the morning of the fourth day, Axie awoke in her room and sensed that the dust from backstage at the Alvin Theater, the vague rumble and small insistent vibrations of the plane on the long flight over the Atlantic and the length of Europe, all of these and many other strains had seeped out of her, and she found herself refreshed, and eager to explore this strange place. First of all, what kind of a guest room was this? It was long and wide, with a high pointed ceiling, and shuttered windows on three of the walls. Her bed, rather narrow and high, stood at the far end, there was a huge old armoire, and not a great deal else. There was a little table by her bed and on the table a hand bell. She had used it before, and now she tinkled it again.

Instead of the woman in black, Maria, who had been bringing her breakfast, Spyro burst in after a minute or two. "No more breakfast in bed," he said firmly, "come out on the balcony for a cup of nice instant Nescafé with Lambros and me."

"What about orange juice?"

He frowned at her. "There aren't any oranges on Paxos."

"Bacon and eggs?"

"*Bacon and eggs?* Where do you think you are, at the Algonquin?"

Axie put on a white robe and slippers, hurriedly brushed her hair, cast one eagle glance at herself in the one small mirror in the room, was relieved that at least she now looked rested, and followed Spyro out of the room. It was characteristic of the peculiar intimacy which existed between them that Spyro did not leave the room while she did these routine and yet intimate tiny morning rituals. She had no secrets from him. He had undoubtedly sensed her affair with Doug. He had also undoubtedly hated it. He did not hate her; he hated *it*. Axie was aware of this, but she simply continued to act with Spyro as though she were not. They *acted* together, played to one another. Knowing about and hating her affair with Doug, Spyro nevertheless wished to continue their lifelong private comedy-drama. Had she any doubts of this, the invitation to Paxos had banished them.

Coming out onto the terrace, she felt struck and swept up into the natural marvel of Greece, and the summer, and the Aegean. From the outer edge of the terrace, with its potted geraniums, from this level of the house there was a sheer drop of seventy feet or so to the sea, where little whitecaps this morning sprang up in the blue-green water. The sun played down upon this balcony and upon the sea, and a Godlike pure sky spread overhead.

In wrought-iron chairs around a wrought-iron table Spyro and Lambros indicated for her to join them in what passed for breakfast: instant coffee, mineral water, bread, butter, marmalade.

"Where are the blueberry pancakes?" she inquired.

"Oh shut up," said Spyro. She felt right at home.

"Well then, where are your parents?"

"Athens. How do you feel?"

"Splendid. At last."

"Good. Today you can explore the island."

"How will we see it? On foot? Or—"

"Not we, sweetheart. Lambros and I are taking the seaplane to Piraeus, meeting Dad, and then taking the plane back. We'll rendezvous back here for dinner. Then we're all going out dancing. Greek dancing. They won't let you dance in the tavernas here because you're ugly and a woman, and only beautiful graceful men are allowed to dance. You watch, over in the corner with all the ugly women in shawls."

Axie gazed at him, gave him her faraway smile. Finally, in a toned-down version of that voice which made every syllable heard at the top of the second balcony, she said, "Screw you, darling. If I want to dance, I will dance. The men will like it. The men will love it. It all depends on how *I* feel about it. Judging from the music I've been hearing coming out of the kitchen, I won't feel inspired to get on my feet and entertain them. Why is it such depressing music?"

"But it's not depressive," put in Lambros in his low voice. "Not at all. You don't understand it yet, because you've never seen anybody dance to it. It's for dancing. You'll see, tonight. Sorry we have to leave you alone all day on your first day out and about."

"Oh well of course I do want to sightsee around the island."

"There's a carriage coming for you at ten o'clock," said Spyro. "At the end of the drive give him forty drachmas, no more and no less. Do you have any Greek money?"

She shook her head. Both brothers quickly reached into their pockets and deposited a pile of bills in front of her.

Axie sat back in her chair and, drawing a deep breath of the crystalline sea air, surveyed her new world. Before and below her stretched the dazzling sea, and gazing up in the opposite direction she saw the slope rising steeply on to the bare summit—a mile away? Three miles? It was impossible for her to judge, so clear was the air, so sharply outlined was all she beheld on the slope and the summit: a white monastery at the crest, the slender, graceful cypresses rising near it, and two donkeys carrying two people approaching the monastery.

The sun was striking the raw wall, cliff, which rose to the right of the little trail leading up to the monastery, and something about the way this ruthlessly clear sunlight struck that raw, reddish wall of cliff made Axie sense that she had never, never seen anything so bizarre, so far from her world, so, well, Martian or Venutian or otherworldly. It was very beautiful in its starkness, but infinitely strange and remote and foreign.

How did I ever come to be here, she asked herself wonderingly. The answer promptly came: because you became intimate friends with Spyro and the Talouris family, and they brought you here, and they did that because they care for you and want you near them, and there is something special in you that people want near them, sitting in a wrought-iron chair having breakfast with them, or across footlights, in the same theater with them.

Well, she reflected, if that is the reason things like this happen to me, then thank God for giving me whatever it is he has given me so that I have moments like this, here staring at that extraordinary wall of reddish cliff under that sunlight, a sight that in the ordinary course of things I would never behold, never be sitting here gazing at in mystification. But I am here and I am looking at it, and because of that, just that, that sight I see before me, I will never be quite the same. I'm richer for this, and if I go on acting, if people continue to want to see me, I will have more to bring to them, because of this.

At ten o'clock Axie came into the entrance hall, which was two stories high and paved with tan marble. The carriage driver, a wiry middle-aged island man, was standing just inside the front door waiting for her. The double front doors, great mahogany slabs with big brass fittings, were opened for her by him, and Axie, feeling a little queenly in spite of herself, swept through and out into the carriage which waited just outside, on the cobblestone way. It was a black, open, one-horse four-wheeler. The driver got up in front, and they creaked off.

The sun was very definitely shining that morning, as every summer morning. She put on a large straw garden hat she was carrying, one of Norma's.

"Where're we going?" she asked, to make conversation.

"*Ya-su,*" he answered, and gave the same answer to

a couple of other attempts by her to start conversation. So Axie settled back on the worn leather cushioning and let herself roll along, like Queen Victoria.

The cobbled way began to curve upward toward a ridge, with whitewashed little houses and sheds and a tiny shop or two on both sides. There were people and cats here and there, and both groups glanced at her with the same very casual interest. At the top of the little rise the carriage started a gentle descent and there, spread before her, was an interior upland of surpassing beauty.

The late morning sun was flooding over a wide rolling sweep of green highland, illuminating groves of olive trees and cypresses; hanging in the air was the smell of broom and Spanish chestnuts, of wildflowers and leaves, and there was an undertone of bees in unison, and even a brook with clear water sliding by. Axie knew this was unusual, in the parched Greek islands. Paxos was exceptional. So were the Talourises, and this was their island.

Fan-topped Mediterranean pines lined the little road, and the cottages and shops which had been beside it now gave way to open country, with just small clusters of white cube houses here and there, and square white dovecotes. Strung along a ridge in the middle distance was a white village, with several light blue domes seeming to float over it. Tamarisk trees with knobby trunks and feathery fernlike leaves were scattered among the olives and cypresses and pines; bursts of flowers appeared here and there in the earth and in urns next to cottage doorways. As her carriage swayed slowly into the village the arctic whiteness of the cubist houses surrounding her made Axie feel she had drifted into some other world, but not a threatening world, a magical one, and safe.

When her carriage reached the small central square she saw on the other side of it a brilliantly white Byzantine church of many arches, with two white bell towers beside and detached from it, each with two levels of arches and a silver dome, up against the depthless blue sky. The church itself had a much larger silver dome, set against the immaculate blue sky.

This is the most enchanting place I have ever been in my life, she murmured to herself in a quiet, intense inner voice.

Curiously, there was no one to be seen, except for one woman hanging out the wash on a balcony, and one man riding sidesaddle on a donkey crossing the square.

Her driver stopped the carriage. Perhaps he thought she would like to go into the church and pray, she reflected. But Axie did not want to go indoors on this sun-washed morning, and she felt that in a sense she was already praying, if by prayer you meant deep appreciation of life and what has been put on earth, and gratitude for all of it.

I will never be anywhere more beautiful, she thought. This is one of the great moments of my life. I should not be passing through this moment alone, however; I should not be passing through this moment alone. And as the driver, sensing that this foreign woman, who doubtless belonged to one of those Protestant cults, was not going to perform her reverences within Saint Demetrios, turned the carriage slowly back toward the road on which they had come, this thought burned into Axie's mind slowly and deeply: I should not be passing through this divine experience alone.

23

Spyro and Lambros were back from the mainland by dinnertime, and the three of them dined together in the central courtyard of the agglomeration of little buildings which, combined, made up the Talouris home. It was paved with tan fieldstone, on different levels and with little walls and potted geraniums and tamarisk trees and bougainvillea climbing, and an air, people thought, of quiet elegance. The amphorae which divers had found on the floor of the sea nearby, graceful, chalk-colored amphorae from antiquity, bearers of wine and oil from the mainland to one of the Homeric islands, these stood in cast-iron supports for the pointed bases in the courtyard. There were cast-iron tables and long cushioned chairs and candles behind hurricane glass and an atmosphere, here more than anywhere else in the house or anywhere else on the island, of luxurious withdrawal. In one corner there was an orange copper Turkish brazier on a ruby rug, and a bubble pipe.

Here Axie, in a blue linen dress, and the Talouris brothers, in slacks and white embroidered loose Greek island shirts, ate quietly. The food was simple, the wine resinated. Axie had never tasted it before, and after the initial surprise at its bite, she decided that she liked this wine, that it went well with this food. Lambros looked dark and hawklike in the candlelight, far more Greek than Spyro with his high, somewhat Scottish coloring. To look at them you would not guess that they were brothers, or even half-brothers. They did, however, seem to get on well, for the reason that Lambros appeared to be, along with their father, one of the handful of people whom Spyro respected, and even deferred to, a little.

They discussed the shipping business, and then they talked about the sparse fishing in these waters, and the way the sponge business here was dying out, how the divers on Kalymnos had to go farther and farther toward Africa each year to bring in even a minimal harvest. The talk drifted to the problem of getting more water for the inhabitants of Paxos, and whether foreigners, especially Americans, would come to an island where the public accommodations were so simple, and as the conversation went its quiet, interested way Axie drifted into a realization that the New York theater and the Hollywood movie industry were rapidly losing reality for her; it felt to her as she sat in the candlelight fondling her wine glass that they did not in any concrete way exist but were instead illusions just like the artifacts, plays and movies, which they produced. Not only was *The Children's Hour* an illusion but so was the Alvin Theater and Forty-fifth Street and the Theater Guild and Broadway. Donkeys and a water shortage and olive trees and sponges were on the other hand very real.

As the evening went on, the light faded from the faultless sky, and stars pierced through as darkness deepened toward black. Soon the black canopy above them appeared to be just that, a canopy, with tiny holes pierced by an ice pick—the stars—hinting at the glorious endless blaze of god-light behind and above this black canopy.

A little later, all of them somewhat bemused by a cool, huge moon beginning to peer down upon them from behind the monastery on the ridge, they made their way through the connected living rooms to the big entrance hall and out onto the cobbled way, not turning right as Axie had done in the carriage this morning, but left along a track hanging above the sea, toward the little fishing village where boats from the mainland arrived. As they strolled along this track cutting through the coastal palisades of Paxos, the lights of other distant islands could be seen off in the darkness: closer by, a tiny motor launch puttered slowly across the wide silver sea and on board it some people were singing, one of the convoluted, dirgelike songs of Greece.

Then they reached their destination: a kind of nightclub in a one-story stone building where small boats had been built until recently. There was one still there, suspended from the ceiling, and another, upside down, served as a bar. From one corner came the wailing, half-Oriental music of Greece. A man was playing a bouzouki—a variation of the mandolin—another fiddled, and the third played a bagpipe made from the skin of a goat.

They sat down at a battered, square little wooden table and ordered a bottle of wine. Nobody paid any particular attention to them. The floor was concrete: a few naked light bulbs gave illumination here and there.

"This is the greatest and most elegant nightclub on Paxos," Spyro explained.

Men were sitting at the other tables, and no one seemed to be drinking much. The women, gathered by themselves in one part of the room, wore simple cotton dresses and had their hair frizzed in the style of the 1930s; the men, naturally without jackets in the summer heat, went in for more contrast. One young man had on a pair of chocolate-

brown slacks, black shirt, silver necktie, black and white
striped socks and large white shoes. He had a lot of hair
and a long pencil mustache over his wide, white smile.
Another man, older, undersized, in purple shirt and blue
pants, got up to dance by himself. As he took the floor he
looked as though he was unhappy and a failure. And then
he began to dance to the sensual music, and suddenly over
his tired face there came a charmed, slow smile, and into
his thin body came a swaying, pumping grace; out of this
middle-aged man a happy faun was emerging, he was
moving with a slow and easy passion, with a kind of
knowledgeability, a worldliness.

Axie, leaning close to Lambros as though some of the
Greeks might overhear, asked, "Where in the world did
he learn to dance like *that*?"

"From the music. Just by listening to it and doing
what it tells him. Now do you think the music is depressing?"

She turned back toward the floor, onto which the
young man with the silver necktie was now moving. "I'm
beginning to understand what the music is all about," she
murmured. Arms extended, hands hanging down and
snapping up, he danced with his head down, concentrating
on some spot on the floor, advancing toward it, drawing
back, circling it, trying, it seemed to Axie's intent eyes,
to win it, charm, hypnotize it. He danced for about five
minutes without ever repeating himself, without noticing
the people around him, who weren't noticing him either;
the only relationship now was between the dancer and the
spot on the floor.

At last he seemed satisfied; he had communicated
whatever it was. There was naturally no applause. He hadn't

been dancing for anyone else; no one except Axie had paid much attention. He went back to his table and took a sip of wine.

What kind of people are these, she wondered to herself intently. They are so carefree one moment, so concentrated the next. Everything is so rudimentry and simple in this dance room—it was impossible to think of it as a "nightclub"—and yet there is a powerful underlying sophistication. No one is deceived about anything around here.

The dancing went on and grew wilder: men began to dance holding not-that-small tables in their jaws; people casually tossed plates which shattered beneath their feet; a large older man performed an explicit kind of belly dance, bumps, grinds, everything; two young men appeared to seduce each other on the dance floor and then wandered away in different directions, as though unaware of the implications of their dance.

But Axie did not believe that anyone here was unaware of anything. "Why don't you guys dance," she suddenly demanded of Spyro and Lambros, "either alone or else together?"

Lambros's rather hooded eyes gazed into hers. "We're self-conscious, see? We've been to Paree and New York and Beverly Hills. We just can't get up and do it that way now because—"

Spyro cut in: "We wonder what people will think. Think now. I used to dance here once in a while when I was a kid. But now, too self-conscious. I guess you're right," he said across her to Lambros. "But you," his penetrating eyes turned back upon her, "you said you were going to dance. So go on. Get up there."

Axie had by now appeared hundreds of times before audiences, and although she was always tense and keyed up before a performance, she no longer suffered from stage fright. Now she was suddenly stricken with fear at the mere suggestion that she might go out onto the swath of bare concrete, move to that music before these thirty or forty people. "*I* don't know how to dance to that," she muttered.

"And even if you did?" prompted Spyro knowingly.

She paused, and then said forthrightly, "You're right. Even if I knew some steps, I wouldn't do it, here. The women aren't dancing. But I don't think even that is the reason. I just wouldn't . . . dare. I—I don't know why. Too far from home." That raw wall of cliff she had gazed up at this morning in wonder, that great reddish slab which said: You are in another world. Destiny never expected *you* to be *here*. This is alien to you and you are alien to it . . .

That recollection was thrilling to her in a bizarre way, but it also created a kind of chill at the back of her mind, and a warning.

24

Mornings were unromantic on Paxos, not to look at but to hear. For the next three mornings, as every morning since her arrival, Axie was flung into at least momentary wakefulness by the crazy crowing of a cock somewhere, and then a mad answering crow, another, another. They hurled their cries across the fields and hills, and soon after

them the first donkey would pass along the way outside
the house, pause to bray in some terrible agony, and then
pass on. A little church bell somewhere reasserted sanity
and order by tinkling remindingly, and another Paxian day
had commenced.

Axie sat up, stretched, and rang her own little table
bell. Maria, small and dark in a black dress, soon came in
with what was apparently the one and only breakfast: mineral water, Nescafé, bread, butter, marmalade.

People starved to death during World War Two on
this island, Axie reminded herself, so shut up.

Maria placed the tray on the little table beside her bed
and then opened the three shutters on the wall to her left,
the two shutters on the wall behind her bed, and the three
shutters on the long glass doors to her right.

"What a beautiful day!" exclaimed Axie rhetorically.

"Yes," commented Maria.

Not much English had come out of Maria as yet. "Are
Lambros and Spyro up?" she ventured on.

"Oh yes. Gone to Athens."

"What? Already? So early?"

"Mr. Talouris send message for them to come back.
Business, important."

"When will they be back?"

"Tonight. Maybe. Maybe tonight."

So Axie resigned herself to that. She would have another day to sightsee, although once again she would be
alone.

Not being able to share it with someone you loved
or even liked was a kind of desecration.

Next to her room there was a narrow, high bathroom
and standing in the tub she took a very brief shower with

a hand-held spray. Water was short on Paxos: even for the Talourises it was not to be wasted, not a drop of it.

Then she dressed in a white cotton shirtwaist dress with a full skirt, put on some sandals, took one of Norma's wide-brimmed hats, and sat down on the balcony overlooking the sea—a magic place on a magic morning—and wrote a few letters home. There was more to this than doing her duty, doing what her parents and Douglas Shore and her lifelong friend Madge would expect of her. She was keeping in touch with them, with the past, with her roots, reaching out, almost nervously, to reassure herself that they were there, five thousand miles away but nevertheless there, palpable. She would not have felt quite so isolated, and, gazing around over her shoulder for a minute at the raw, reddish, huge slab of featureless cliff, in quite such an alien environment, if there had been a telephone in the house and the possibility had existed of calling up her American relatives and friends, her American past. But she could not: there were no telephones on Paxos. True, the ship-to-shore telephone in the *Pacificus* could be routed through Athens and then presumably on to America, but the *Pacificus* was not here: she was in Glyfada, the little port near Athens, and Stamos and Norma were living aboard her while he conducted this pressing business there.

It was about eleven in the morning when Axie decided to walk along past that "nightclub" to the tiny fishing village beyond and mail her letters. She told this to Maria, said she would have lunch in one of the three little restaurants there—Maria seemed to look quizzical about this plan, as though there were anything out of the ordinary in it—and Axie set off.

The village was perhaps three-quarters of a mile away,

and beneath her big hat she was not uncomfortable under the downpouring sunshine because she had noticed, and now emulated, the gait of the Paxiots. Settling back a little on her hips, she strolled along with smooth, very unhurried deliberation, letting her arms rotate a little with each step, her weight moving smoothly, effortlessly from hip to hip. In this way she ambled along the dusty track above the sea and down into the village.

After mailing her letters, she sat down at a square wooden table in a little outdoor restaurant under a great square awning and ordered a lunch of fish and salad and white wine.

There were only eight or ten other people having lunch, all of them with the look of visitors to Paxos, dressed not like islanders but Athenians. The waiters seemed to be noticing her; she began to feel conspicuous. She alone was neither an Athenian nor a Paxiot; she was instead a star of stage and screen, and What, a voice she almost heard bouncing off the slab of red cliff seemed to demand, does *that* mean?

Maybe I'm getting a little too much sun, big hat or no big hat, she muttered to herself.

The lunch began to revive her, however, and the wine to stimulate her. Suddenly a gust of wind plunged across the waterfront, driving the big canvas awning over the restaurant wildly back and forth on its guide wires, and then drifting away again and leaving calmness behind. Axie went on eating. Abruptly another gust hurled itself across the agora toward the restaurant; this time a waiter was standing next to the awning, and he grabbed it. A moment later he found himself ten feet in the air, and he swung there for a few moments while the other waiters and the

Athenians shouted with laughter. Then he fell swinging back to earth, breathing heavily but with a game grin.

The sun was not alone in ruling these islands; it shared dominance with such obstreperous winds as these, which were capable of any vagary. Calmness and heavy sunshine returned to the scene. Axie paid for her lunch to a waiter who seemed to be amused by her in some way, and started in her slow, Paxiot stroll across the paving stones, marblelike slabs, in the sun. She did not want to go back to the house at once, and so she continued to the far end of the waterfront. Here another dirt and pebble track rose gradually along the shore palisades past a small abandoned stone fort toward open country. She decided to go a little way along it before turning back; after all, she was not even a mile from the Talouris house, and the heat and sunshine, while very strong, were not very oppressive; it was a dry hotness, welcoming, reassuring, life-giving.

There was no possibility that she would faint, and in any case she wasn't the fainting type. Soon she would go back to the house and have a nap, and then go down the outside steps to the sea beneath the house for a late-afternoon swim.

She was trying to feel comfortable in this place, on this island. It was Spyro's and Lambros's spiritual home, and although the thought that she would before very long marry Lambros had never yet entered her head, still she knew of this family's importance to her. This bond had been and would continue to be lifelong; she sensed that. And here all around her was the family's basic dimension— not Greek merely, but very specifically Paxiot—this island, these palisades, this place. She sensed that she had fallen in love with Paxos, and like certain loves this new passion inspired fear in her, because it meant a surrender on her part, and a vulnerability.

The two huge gusts which had swept across the agora presaged a rising wind, and although she was in the lee of the hill behind her and could not feel it, she could see this wind ruffling the blue, blue sea below into festive white-caps. She drew a deep breath, tingled with pleasure; what a magical place.

There had been a faint buzzing sound in the distance gradually growing louder and more specific, and now around the curve of the track ahead of her a small motorcycle appeared, and as it drew closer she saw a burly young man wearing a cap, a sun- and windburned young man who was grinning a little as he pulled up alongside her, slowing to a stop.

He made some pleasant remark in Greek, smiling, and began to fan himself rather comically with his cap. Doubtless his remark had just been about the heat.

"*Ya-su*," commented Axie, for that was all she could say in Greek, and even that she did not know the meaning of. It was shameful that she had been here a week and still knew no other word.

That word made him grin a little more widely; her accent, and for that matter her appearance, probably made it clear that she was not a Greek.

Then he arched his neck toward the little passenger seat behind him and said something that was surely, "Get on."

Axie stood and she blinked. He was burly and he was healthy and his smile was beginning to be irresistible and she was five thousand miles away and that slab of wall had some strange, opaque meaning for her and she was nobody here and she wanted badly to get on that little seat on his motorcycle.

So she did. Her full skirt made it easy to straddle the machine and, as he started forward rather suddenly, she had to fling her arms around his taut waist. He turned the machine skillfully in the dirt track in a half-circle and headed it back toward the open country. And it was open here, treeless, verging on desertlike with low scrub growth and many protruding rocks, stones on the track making the motorcycle ride rough going, and how did you say "Turn around and go back?" but soon he was turning off the main track onto a little side path in a steep little valley, raw, stony, dusty, empty. Here he stopped, turned, and gave her a grin.

Axie got off the motorcycle and so did he, kicking out a little stand to hold the machine upright.

They faced each other. There was a short mustache over his wide smile, a straight, well-shaped, rather long nose, and he did not look typically Greek; his eyes were bright and smiling and greenish, and his hair, falling out from under his cap, was dark blond. Above all, he was full of confidence and Axie was stripped of every vestige of that, had been since coming in contact with this island.

There was a deafening silence in her ears, and, breathless, she looked carefully into his eyes. Then he advanced, still with that winning, warming smile, put his workman's arms around her and gently, persistently forced his tongue into her mouth. There was a smell of garlic about him, and of strong Mediterranean cigarettes. These odors mingled with his faint sweatiness to undermine her. *You tease* reverberated out of her early days with Doug; you came here with this man, didn't you? He said get on and you did—and now she and this man were getting down just where they stood, down onto the track, and there was reddish dust rising thinly past her hair around her face, and the clothes dividing her secret body from his were gone, and he was entering her with the same confidence she saw in his grin—You are not going to resist, because it is pleasure—and she went with it and with him in the reddish, thin dust under this sky. The man drove Axie into a displacement of her ordinary self; he thrust her to some disjointed level free of fear and of hope too: she was shoved bluntly out of herself, she was insulted, she was violated; she embraced this fiercely, she fought with it, went with it, loved it. She was wrecked; she was buoyed on a wave of deep confidence.

When—and they must have been there a long time—he slowly pulled away from her she thought: Now I face the worst moment of my life—but he got up, smiling, pulling his clothes together, glancing down to see that she would do the same, and Axie got to her feet and rearranged her clothes, and brushed as much of the dust from her dress and her hair as she could, and with shaky hands put Norma's hat back on her head, and began to say to herself, I'm in a daze, and this is all a dream, and then corrected: No, my mind is clear and everything happened because I let it happen and wanted it to happen, and there are no excuses and I wasn't even remotely drunk and I was not sunstruck, I was in control of myself and he forced nothing upon me; all he really did was say "Get on" and the rest followed from that, naturally. He just did what we both wanted him to do; he did it, and I did it.

They climbed back on the motorcycle, and he returned her to a spot past where they had met, beside the old abandoned fort, just short of the village.

He smiled, confidently, once more, she gave him a tentative wave of the hand, and then she strode off, the Alexandra Reed stride, one of her trademarks. Sweat then broke out around her head and she thought it was a delayed reaction to the outrageousness of what she had just done, panic now setting in, and then she realized—No, that's not why I'm breaking into a sweat; it's simply because I'm walking too fast, that stride will never do here. So, forcing herself, she settled back into the easy, Paxiot gait she had learned, and, ambling along in this fashion under the fullness of the afternoon sun, feeling broken, and feeling a part of this island, reeling inwardly, she returned to the Talouris house.

25

Axie was rather silent at dinner that night, which was otherwise much like the dinner four days earlier, just herself and Lambros and Spyro in the courtyard; and she had very little to say during the next days when both brothers were free to enjoy themselves, and the diversions were swimming and lying in the sun and waterskiing and scuba diving.

This last activity, which she was trying for the first time, was the sole experience she could really bear in these strange days; not only could she bear it, she came to welcome it, look forward to it, treasure it. Diving was in some way linked to the man and the motorcycle and the bare sun and the reddish dust, the all-too-real hallucination of what had happened, so bluntly, so brusquely, that afternoon.

The memory of what she had done, of what they had done together, she and this nameless man, was nerve-wracking, but nerve-wracking at one remove. It was a shock, but also a reinforcement to her. She felt threatened, and she also felt safer, more secure, in turmoil and with a new calmness.

Axie was beginning to think that she was not exactly ashamed of it. She was shaken to the core by what she had done, because the woman who had said "*Ya-su*" and gotten onto that little seat on the motorcycle and the woman who had so unresistingly sunk down into that reddish dust, and then afterward gotten up from it, as matter-of-factly as he had gotten up, rearranging her clothes and brushing off as much of the dust as possible, that woman was not based on any prior knowledge of herself. Axie was the one who had not stumbled when going over the New England stone wall with Spyro, the woman who had stopped short of all other sexual completion until Douglas Shore, who was making the career she had dreamed of possible, had shown that this was what he fundamentally wanted of her. Then at last, in just the right New England state, just the right inn in that state, finally, Axie Reed had given in.

Given in. Even that concept was wrong, she now was able to feel. She had given in to Douglas Shore. How ridiculous. But that's the way she had seen it then. Douglas truly loved her, and she knew he was never disappointed in her. But still, her feelings had all been wrong and stupid and ignorant.

She was no longer, as she reflected during these vacation days on Paxos, ashamed of what had happened, but she wondered who this newly revealed woman was. Axie was not going to become a promiscuous tramp, surely, surely not that. But she was not going to be the woman who had arrived on this island any more either. Something had emerged, some demand she made, urgency.

Sitting, coping with all these thoughts and anxieties on the terrace above the sea one day after lunch, alone, Lambros and Spyro having gone elsewhere, she turned rather reluctantly to gaze up at the reddish, almost featureless slab of a cliff above her. It was an oracle, her own private Greek oracle, and it was completely voiceless, could say nothing, as inexpressive as anything on earth, an immovable, almost blank slab of rock. And it always confronted her, always would, here.

All the same, who in God's name am I and how could I have done that with that green-eyed man, she began to demand of herself again, a feverish inner voice welling up as she pulled her eyes away from that alien cliff and stared down at her hands—long, slender, lady's hands—I don't know his name and we had not a word of any language in common and can anything be kept secret on an island as small as this one? Did he know I was staying in this house?

No, she reflected a little less tautly, he didn't. He would have acted differently if he'd known I was connected to the mighty Talourises: he would have made his overture, my being here with the rich people wouldn't have stopped him, but he would have done so more carefully, with more guile. No, he simply thought I was a lone, stray visitor staying at the tiny hotel in the village: that restaurant where I had lunch, it's connected to the hotel. Did he go by on his motorcycle just about the time I was ordering lunch? I think perhaps I remember that a motorcycle did go by then.

He took me for a lone and lonely English girl, or a Scandinavian come from the frozen north of Europe for sexual adventure, as so many Northern European girls and women do, and I suppose always have done since the decline and fall of the Roman Empire: I was to him one of those lone, yearning Northerners and he liked the look of me and decided, then and there, to be kind to me, give me what I had come for.

And so, he did.

But I am not a Northern European and had not come here for that, never dreamed of anything like that happening here.

But I was scared. This island had scared me, those sensual men dancing had unnerved me, that damn overhanging cliff had threatened me, and so when he was suddenly there I went into his arms and let him into my body. I propitiated this island with him.

And now maybe I'm pregnant, and the father is a Paxiot—fisherman? Olive-grower? I don't even know. Cold sober I walked into this, putting my future, my career, everything at risk. Did that man dream of taking precautions? Don't be ridiculous. Women who come like that to the Mediterranean must take their chances.

So the tremulous thoughts flowed through Axie's mind, but this last fear, that she might be pregnant, did not take root. She didn't think so; she simply didn't believe it could happen. She and Douglas did not always take precautions and nothing had happened, and she somehow felt sure nothing would happen.

I'll get pregnant when I want to, and not before, she

asserted inwardly. And then a wry thought: Well, humiliated in the red dust or not, my arrogance is still intact. Maybe I couldn't be an actress without it.

At five that afternoon she and Spyro and Lambros went scuba diving again off the rocks beneath the Talouris house. Axie was good at various sports, notably water sports, and she quickly adapted herself in the world of the undersea, the weightless world, the graceful, slowed world of the depths—for the Talouris boys were not ones to fool around when they were armed with kick fins and an air tank and a face mask and a spear, and down they plunged, Axie trailing gamely behind, past fifty feet, past sixty, past seventy, realizing as she went that she was rapturously happy, because on this gorgeous and threatening island she had made sexual love with a green-eyed man without exchanging a word, without being able to, a man she would never see again, an act she would never duplicate: maybe he had been a god, or an imp, or a devil: but no, devils did not exist in pagan Greece, did they?

SIX

26

Still the sunstruck days continued. The press of business which had repeatedly called Lambros and Spyro to the mainland had apparently ceased or had at least been suspended; they now appeared to have little to do.

"Holiday time at last," observed Lambros contentedly, as he lay in swimming trunks beside Axie on the flat rock just a few feet above the sea beneath the house.

She pulled her head up a little, a scarf around her hair, wearing dark glasses, to look at him as he lay prone. "Don't you and Spyro want more company here then? You both have been working hard the whole time I've been here, and as far as I can see for months before that in New York."

Don't you want to ask some people, some friends to come, make a house party?"

He opened one eye, a very dark eye, to look at her. "Do you?"

"Oh me," she settled back down on her towel, "well no. But then I've been doing a play for two months. *I* want a little peace and quiet. But that has nothing to do with you and Spyro, you're—"

"Spyro is here to make up his mind whether to get engaged or not—"

That stopped her: her Spyro get engaged? She had met the girl, kind of a hearty girl, from Connecticut. Her Spyro, engaged?

"—and I'm trying to make up my mind," he concluded, and then was silent, and motionless.

"About what?" she asked unguardedly.

"About you."

It was her turn to pause. Then she said in her most controlled voice flatly, "You have to make up your mind about me. I'm puzzling you in some way."

"That you are."

"I don't think I'm so puzzling. Just an actress . . ."

"No," he said a little lazily, "you're quite a bit more than that."

Then it began to seem unmistakable: tautness came into her voice despite herself. "Well we all have different sides to—"

He emitted one rather harsh laugh. "Is *that* what you call it?"

Oh my God, oh the blessed saints and all the oracles of Delphi, has he heard about that man and that day in the dust? Oh lord God Almighty. This tiny island; Greeks, in the village, in this house! Of *course* he knows and so does

Spyro and everyone, she told herself with stiff finality.

Axie compelled a calmness upon herself, and to a certain degree she achieved it. By God I'm an actress, she reflected. "What was that barking laugh all about?" she inquired.

This time he pulled himself up onto his elbows and turned both those nearly black eyes upon her. His face was slightly smiling but otherwise unreadable. "Oh come on, Axie."

She gazed levelly back at him: "What are you talking about?"

Finally having decided something, he said, in a new tone, a shade closer to her, "I never knew you were a very sexual woman. I should have."

Axie had prided herself all of her life on her honesty, and did not think she had often betrayed it. Come what might, she was not going to betray it now. Once again managing to gain control of her voice, she forced herself to say, "You're talking about . . . that man . . . ?"

"Yes," he let drop.

"Nothing like it ever happened before," she added hurriedly. "I was frightened here, too much alone."

"Um-hum."

"You don't believe me."

"I didn't say I didn't believe you."

"Well? Do you?"

There was a silence from this long, lean, athletic, dark-haired man, lying nearly naked beside her, and then he said, "I don't really know. I don't think I've ever met anyone exactly like you. Spyro's the one who really knows you."

She drew an almost gasping breath. "Oh my God, Spyro!"

"Spyro doesn't believe a word and never will and won't let this story be discussed, and he'll never believe any of it unless you tell him it's so."

And that I shall never do, she tensely instructed herself. Withholding this from him is not being dishonest; it is survival, mine, in a way his too. There is honesty, and then there is suicidal self-punishment, and the punishment of those who love you.

Lambros's attitude this morning on this subject was beginning, in spite of her controlled panic, to, in some other cranny of her mind, fascinate her. He was not shocked and he was not denouncing her and he was not even laughing at her. He was interested; he seemed to be intrigued.

She reflected: I think he may come to believe me when I say that such a thing has never happened before, that it struck me from nowhere, or rather from the strangeness of this island, struck me in my solitude, and that it is not me. Is not, and yet is: I did it, I, well, urgently desired that man, and I took him as he took me.

I think that Lambros senses this. And he is in some way not displeased.

For the first time I have truly interested him, intrigued him. I can always feel how people are reacting to me, hundreds of them, even a couple of thousand, all at one time. Surely I cannot be wrong about this one man, a man I know, here with me on this rock.

The rocks of Paxos: so different from the soft, fertile, loamy soil of the East End. They had as much to do with this strange episode as anything; that red dust, what was it except crushed rock? The rock-face of the Aegean, that big rock cliff, the reddish dust, this slab we're lying prone on now under that implacable sun: these rocks weighed on me, and they changed me.

She rolled her head over to look at his hawklike profile. "Now do you think I'm a whore?" she asked. "Have I disgraced your family here on your island? Don't keep me waiting," she went on more shakily, "just tell me straight out."

He drew a breath and then said calmly, "These people on this island have watched their mothers starve. During the war. Sex, there's nothing in sex that's unknown. They have rigid standards of behavior and yet nothing can shock them. You yourself might as well be from Mars, as far as their standards are concerned. They just watch, and they don't really bat an eyelash."

She was staring hard at him: of the two hurdles, she felt she had crossed one with unexpected safety: now the other. "But you—?"

"What do I think?" he repeated her question. He paused, not to torment her with suspense, she felt, but because he really had to seek the answer in himself. He too was going to be dedicated, at least today, to honesty. Then he said in a tone which caught her: "You're an interesting woman, Alexandra. More than I realized." Then the single barking laugh.

And in spite of it, that slicing-through-her laugh, this had been the beginning of their real relationship, and a more bizarre beginning, she felt, may never have occurred. Out of nowhere she had suddenly behaved like the world's most irresponsible tramp, and this man who had been taking her for granted and shown her only the most superficial attention was now intrigued by her.

But that's the way it was.

"I've known a lot of women," he said with a kind of sigh some days later when they were alone on the breakfast balcony. "All kinds. I travel everywhere. You know. I've known a lot of women."

Maria came to remove their coffee cups. Maria, however unblinkingly the Paxiots were supposed to accept the behavior of "Martians" like herself, now treated her in a new way: Maria rather crept when around Axie, something guarded and pantherish coming into her movements.

Lambros has never known, Axie confided to herself, someone just like me: good family, good schools, good breeding, good career, suddenly violating all by getting down into the dust with some strange man. It's set him off thinking about me, hasn't it? He's intrigued. Perhaps he was getting a little jaded. And now I've presented him with something very different and I suspect, I just begin to suspect, that he's becoming fascinated.

Although of course she encountered him, Spyro made himself scarce during these days, it seemed to Axie. In this complicated rambling building that was entirely possible. "You are never to tell him I admitted anything!" Axie had ended her conversation on the rock with Lambros by issuing this order, her voice now a growl, her eyes boring into him. Lambros, as much as he could while lying prone on a rock, shrugged easily. "If that's what you want. Not a word. To him, or to anyone."

Axie's eyes narrowed a little as she thought: I can trust you, Lambros Talouris. I know that I can. Maybe it is because there is a basic indifference about you, maybe because you are somewhat world-jaded; whatever it is, wherever this springs from, I can take you at your word.

And so she did not jump out of her skin when, days

later, rounding a white corner of the house, she almost collided with Spyro. They both stood still, staring. "Come," she said in her warm voice, taking his arm, "let's go up on the top of the house. I know there's a platform there. I've never seen it. You show it to me."

He gave a final, rather sidelong glance into her eyes and then murmured, "Okay. You ought to see it."

They mounted several flights of interior stone stairs, and, surrounded by the whitewashed walls, Axie once again became conscious of the stoniness of Paxos, so ungiving and so unforgiving, the rock of the world.

The final narrow little steps were on the outside of the building and then they emerged onto a plain square space surrounded by a low white wall, containing two little iron chairs, a little iron table, and nothing else.

What was there was the view. The world, at least this world, was spread beneath them, the sea reaching glitteringly away to the distant, hovering islands, the dirt and pebble way leading past the front door and the palisades to the tiny, toylike harbor with the table where she had had lunch, and then rising again past the ruined fort to make a turn around a low hill which concealed the exact spot where she and the man had burned their lusts together; behind them at the top of the long hard bare slope was the placid white monastery and to the right of that the blank reddish slab of cliff confronted her in its massive inscrutability once again, and to the right of that the little way she had taken in the carriage rose to the crest of the hill and disappeared into the enchanted valley beyond.

Above all of course, the bluest and purest and hugest dome of sky in the world spread back and away toward infinity.

Axie sank into one of the chairs. Spyro, in loose gray

cotton slacks and a T-shirt, paced over to one corner and gazed down toward the broken-looking roofs and terraces and tiny balconies and occasional towers of the village.

Axie found the height, the space, the heat and the beauty literally breathtaking. She didn't think she could speak, and if she could, what would she say to this man who had loved her all of his life?

Then he turned. Spyro was the only person in the world she knew who could be more direct than she. "There are sex stories going around about you—"

She drew a breath. Training once again came to her rescue: "Yes, I know there are." Axie believed only she herself could hear the tiny tremor in her voice. "Nobody apparently has anything better to do on this island than gossip. Some man from the village brought me back on his motorcycle when I went too far on the track. Nice man. But I guess people here aren't used to a woman accepting a ride."

Spyro looked at her unreadably. "They said he was bragging in the tavernas that he had sex with you, just like that, down in the dirt, right off, no talk. Just sex. That's what he was bragging about in the tavernas, I hear."

"He," she murmured, forced to get the prevailing conditions known, despite the risk, "didn't—brag about—this to you himself?"

Spyro kind of reared up: "No. He's off the island. He bragged and then he went."

Axie leaned back, stretched slightly. "They've got it all wrong. He gave me a lift. No idea who I was. No interest. Some Swedish tourist. Then somebody must have told him I was staying with the great Talourises. So then he, apparently to make himself important, he made up that—outrageous story you heard. To make himself important."

Spyro paused, and started to thrust his hands characteristically in his pockets, only to find that these pants had none. He shifted his weight. "You know?" he said intensely, squinting in sudden rage. "That's what these peasants here always try to do, make themselves important. That's their way! Anything to be notable!"

"Even slandering me."

Spyro paced diagonally across the space. "If I get my hands on that rotten son-of—" he growled.

Axie got up and crossed to him, put her arm around his neck, nuzzled him a little. "Forget it, darling. What can it mean, here? A little man tries to be important . . ." and as she said these words, too defiant of the gods and the reddish cliff, into her mind's eye was thrust the spare powerful body of that blond workman, looming, all shoulders and chest, blackly over her, sun blazing around him. "He . . ." she pushed lightly, uncertainly on, "isn't anybody. Nothing. Just talk . . . and . . . nothing." She sank down on the outer wall, her back resolutely to the cliff, her face toward the jewel-field of the Aegean.

Spyro paused in his pacing in front of her. "You haven't commented on the view," he said evenly. "Everybody exclaims about the view as soon as they get up here."

"The *view*!" she enthused. "I'm drinking it in, I've been drinking it in. Mesmerizing." And after a final pause, as he slowly resumed his pacing, Axie guardedly shot a glance at him to see whether he had accepted this final lie.

How she hated to lie. She was too proud for it, maybe too arrogant for it. Perhaps in a certain final sense she didn't care enough about most others to lie. But for Spyro she lied, through her bright white teeth.

"Come here," she murmured. "Sit down in that other chair. You make me nervous pacing. Good. Now. Tell me about you and—is it Jane?"

He gazed down in front of him. "Jane. Yeah Jane, Janie. What do you, well, what do you think of her?"

"So healthy. Soooo healthy."

He cocked an eye at her. "All right, Axie. Talk about damning with faint praise! You don't like her."

She ran her fingers quickly through her hair. "I didn't say I didn't like her. I don't know her. But tell me, darling, are you going to marry her?"

Spyro was plunged in silence, forearms on knees. Then he looked over at her. "I guess I am. What do you think of it?"

Well, if it's what you want, and she wants, then wonderful. My opinion isn't important.

Those were the words which sprang to mind, but she did not pronounce them: that was too enormous a lie for her to utter. For her opinion was important, deeply important to Spyro, and she knew it.

She reached over and put a hand on his arm. "Darling, I want more—well almost more than anything in the world for *you* to be happy. You believe me?"

He nodded his head, almost unwillingly.

"Well then, I must ask myself if this marriage will do that for you. If it will, I will love . . . Janie, I will make her love me."

He mumbled something. Was it: "And you know how to do that?"

She had no choice but to go on. "Will she fit in your life? All the traveling, all the Greekness. The tight, tight family ties. Not every American girl could. Very few, I think."

He drew a breath. "Yeah, I think so. If I want her to, she'll do that. She'll do anything."

"I see." Axie sat back and gazed in front of her. "I see. She's madly in love. She will do anything you want. But will she continue to do anything you want, I mean, to fit into your special life, ten years after the marriage, and do it happily?"

"I think so. Yes, I think she will."

"Have to ask, sweetheart. Are *you* in love with *her*?"

He paused again—pauses were uncharacteristic of Spyro—and then he murmured, "She fits me. Just about a perfect fit. I'm a very crazy shape. Hardly anybody would."

And I am the one person in the world who understands exactly what you mean, she murmured with a warm glow to herself. Now you are admitting your oddness, your strangeness, your hostility to most of the world, you are admitting that to me. I think this field hockey girl, this Janie, must be right for you.

Then a final question, the practical one. "What about money? She'll do anything for you. The money, the Talouris fortune, that hasn't got anything to do with it?"

"She's rich, her family's rich, maybe richer than we are."

So, Axie said with some subdued satisfaction to herself, Spyro has found someone who appears to be really right for him. How satisfying! And a pang went through her: someone bound tightly to her by love, a bond that went as far back as she could remember, that someone was being torn from her, that wealth—wealth of *feeling,* that potential devotion . . . she was letting it be ripped away. The loss of it! Oh God, pain. And she must do it, and she would do it and she was, she was . . . happy, yes, yes she was happy.

Tears coming up into her eyes, Axie swiftly got up and, moving over to him, kissed him on the cheek, the other cheek, the mouth.

27

Two days later, toward dusk, the *Pacificus,* long, sleek, ice-cream-white, glided with cool deliberation to a point perhaps 150 yards off the house, and dropped anchor. Beneath the great awning aft there were people, Norma and Stamos and crew members, who could be seen getting assembled, organizing luggage and packages preparatory to taking the launch ashore.

At dinner in the center courtyard, as the candleflames danced on wicks behind the hurricane glass, creating lighting which Axie's professional eye knew to be the most flattering possible, they dined, the four members of the Talouris family and herself. She and Norma wore long gowns, pastel and filmy. Blond and creamy-looking, Norma tonight was placidly beautiful, a woman of a certain age, not thin, nineteenth-century buxom, relaxed. The men all looked particularly healthy and had gotten rather formal, wearing dark blazers and, for Stamos, a white silk suit.

It was a beautiful meal, with a marvelous fish, freshly caught, all of the people looking their best, aglow with health, and on this night in carefree spirits. The protracted business which Stamos had been negotiating from the *Pacificus* in the harbor at Glyfada, and which had involved the hurried trips of Spyro and Lambros to the mainland, had been terminated at last very successfully. Stamos was relaxed. This in itself was an unusual state for him. Within the week he would be urgently pursuing some new goal, increasing his influence, in Greece, in Western Europe, in the United States, in South America, in Japan, everywhere. But for this night, Stamos was relaxed.

This released something in Norma. The stage—and the courtyard was a stage, Axie noticed, beautifully proportioned and lighted, with elegant props, and the costumes, tonight at least, excellent, and even an audience: the three serving women in black and the two men in white—the stage tonight was Norma's.

"You'd never know we were on Paxos, sitting here, would you?" The question seemed to be addressed to Axie.

"It's magical," Axie murmured warmly.

"It's quite unreal, utterly out of place I admit, in spite of those amphorae somebody brought up from the sea and—"

"Somebody!" cut in Spyro. "Us!"

"—and that little mosaic in the corner of Poseidon and his trident and a few other genuinely Greek things. I thought we needed something really elegant here, so here it is. But we had to do all kinds of special things to get enough electricity and enough water, and do something about too much sunlight on the fabrics, and on and on. It's all artificial, expensive and artificial. This island is mostly starkness, isn't it, Axie dear? I'm sure you've explored around—not just confined yourself to the village, have you, gone beyond it . . . mm, it's mostly semiarid and almost incredibly poverty-stricken, at least it was when we built here, our coming and some other people, Athenians, have houses all the way round the other side, well Paxos is not quite the desolation of poverty that it was.

"You know that during the war people tore down their houses and sold the materials to the mainland in order to eat? Yes, and those who didn't have a house to tear down well, they . . .

"But everyone just dug in and clawed at this poor soil and fished in that fished-out sea, and one pretty, devout little girl became a leading international, well, prostitute and then built a house for her parents, and the boys went all over the world to make some money and send it back, send it back, regularly, every month, year in, year out, send it back.

"It really couldn't sustain as many lives as lived on it, Paxos couldn't. But . . . they survived. Those who did die just crept away and starved to death, out of sight, silently.

"The rest just clawed and hung on and made it through, fought and suffered and were stripped of everything, gave up everything, but lived."

SEVEN

28

These visions of Paxos flowed through Axie's mind as she gazed across her hospital room at the color photograph of the agora which Spyro had brought. There near the center of the picture was the little restaurant with the big awning where she had had lunch that day; the church was beside it; the little caïques were tied to the wharf in front of it.

She had heard the island was not much changed.

It was so odd; now when she looked at that rather modest, colorful row of little buildings her thoughts and memories of the place were tied not to Spyro, her bonded friend throughout life, and not to the blond-haired workman with the straight nose who had matter-of-factly intervened so crucially in her life, but of course to the confluence of these two masculine presences into one: Lambros.

Dark and rather brooding, a little hollow-cheeked, self-contained, Lambros to Axie had been rather an enigma; she had not known how to respond to him, what he was made of, until that visit to Paxos. There she had learned that he was like the men dancing in the little club, a conventional exterior screening rare inner grace and tenderness, in short a kind of artist. He was like her, far more than Spyro was. He was feeling and emotion and sensitivity tightly controlled. Spyro was ambition and drive and dominance.

Lambros had been like Greek music: it seemed mournful, dirgelike, unlovely; and then she had seen him gliding so swiftly undersea, spear in hand, and this sight had been like the men dancing: a revelation. He was grace and containment and mystery. The man on the motorcycle had carried her fears and her wariness on Paxos away with him. That act had been so gratuitous, outrageous, larcenous, and it had been something she had had to do. After it, Axie had been able to fall in love with Lambros.

Nothing would have happened otherwise. Lambros did not allow himself to fall in love with women; he responded, sometimes, if they first fell in love with him. When it came to love, Axie herself was able to conceal nothing. Soon after the man and the red dust and their lovemaking, that Zeus-bolt from Olympus, or Hades, Axie knew and the Talourises knew that Axie was falling in love with Lambros.

In the autumn following her return from that first visit to the island, the last full Eisenhower autumn of 1959,

Axie was invited to play in *A Streetcar Named Desire* at a university theater in Massachusetts.

A little stunned at this invitation, one she would have rejected out of hand before that Greek interlude, she sat on the floor in her apartment on East Sixty-second Street and read the play. She had seen Jessica Tandy in the role on Broadway, and Vivien Leigh in the role on the screen. She, Axie, play Blanche? It was almost outrageous casting against type: Blanche—fragile, genteel, vain, corrupted, romantic, illusion-addled, dreamy Blanche, played by leggy, straightforward, athletic Axie! But that simplistic Axie was her "image," not herself, not any longer. Within herself, now, she began to believe she might be able to find a Blanche.

Her living room was long and narrow and dark, with an old-fashioned high ceiling and a curved-top nonworking fireplace, rather sparsely furnished in Early American reproductions. Axie, as always when at home, was wearing slacks, black, and a white blouse.

She pored over the lines of the play. There was one line she knew she would never be able to say convincingly, if she did dare and accept this part: "Our grandfathers and fathers and uncles and brothers exchanged the land for their epic fornications." She didn't believe this line, didn't believe that Blanche would have said it that way; it smacked not of Blanche but of playwriting. But it was the only such line in the play.

At the very end of *A Streetcar Named Desire,* one step away from utter ruin and madness, Blanche with a last heartbreaking courage cries: "How strange that I should be called a destitute woman! When I have all these treasures locked in my heart." Then she breaks into sobs.

That Axie knew she could play. That was the heart of the tragedy. For this broken deluded wreck did in fact have treasures, unspent, locked in her heart.

She decided then and there to accept. She knew now how true Blanche's fate could be: a twilight life of shadings, of variables, of pitfalls and comeuppances.

Doug came to read it with her. "Get out of this walk-up apartment," he muttered irritably on arriving. "You're a star now."

"Somebody up there in Massachusetts saw me in the Hellman play and actually thought I could play Blanche. And I somehow think that just possibly I can, now."

A faint wave of dubiousness crossed his face, and then he grasped her by the shoulder. "Of course you can! And I'll be in your corner. They won't want me to direct it, but I'll be in your corner."

Then they read it, Axie as Blanche, Doug as everybody else. At the end of the reading he simply said, almost muttered: "I see, I see." There was now a new dimension to Axie.

Lambros Talouris, who had been taking her out to dinner and dancing and here and there these alive autumnal nights in Manhattan, murmured, "That's interesting," when she mentioned this engagement. Then he managed to arrange to have business in Boston at that time, and to find his way into the suburb and to the university theater, without telling her, to witness her first performance in the role.

Sitting well back in the orchestra, Lambros watched an Axie playing Blanche who seemed slenderer than the young woman he knew, frailer, more feminine, a gossamer creature, the bouncing beach girl submerged into a tensile, driven woman, a wracked woman who seemed to be all possibilities, and all vulnerabilities.

Afterward, backstage, when he peered around the door of her dressing room, she was seated with Douglas holding both of her hands. She turned and looked across at him, in her makeup, still fragile-seeming, and he stared back at her precisely as though Douglas Shore did not exist. Then Doug stood up and the two men shook hands, cordially. Axie that night on the stage had built a bridge from one to the other, an improbable bridge. They had both seen who she was, to her depths, and what it was in her that held them, both of them.

Axie and Lambros were both staying at the Ritz Hotel in Boston, and late the next morning they met in the lobby to take a walk through the raw very-late-fall gusts in the public gardens across the street. "Yes, that was a pretty good performance last night," he began.

Lambros had been educated in America, and his style was offhand understatement. You had to dig to reach the Greek.

Axie was wearing what she called her "movie producer's overcoat," a man's caramel-colored camel's-hair belted coat that was a little too big for her, bought as a semi-joke in Beverly Hills, redolent of vintage Hollywood male authority; Lambros, dressed for a business lunch, wore a dark homburg and an almost black tailored cashmere overcoat. "I look like a fly-by-night beside you," she remarked, ignoring his comment about her performance for the moment.

"You are a fly-by-night."

"So you thought I was 'pretty good.' " There was a chancy edge to her tone.

"Oh, you know. Listen, all right. It's true. I thought you were great. It was a revelation."

Axie's eyes narrowed for a moment. Finally she said,

her voice low, a touch of growl at the edges, "I never got so far into myself as on that stage. That part pulled out everything in me. That's all there is. That's the ultimate me, for good and evil and beyond good and evil and right to the depths and out the other side of insanity and everything in between. Now you've seen it all." They strolled on among the stripped trees and the gracious spaces of the public gardens, crossed the bridge arching over the lagoon where the famous swan boats plied in summer; they roamed along on this gusty day through the heart of this cultured old city, the gracious, unpretentious openness around them, a thoughtful place, removed, and Lambros from time to time was gazing steadily at her with his blackish eyes; she felt what was to come, and was prepared for it and said yes to it, when, as they reached the far side of the gardens, he asked her to marry him.

And thank God, she thought, looking across the hospital room at the photograph, thank God that I did, that I was able to. For it seemed to resolve, for a time did resolve, her knotty, constricting entanglement with the theater and her ambitions and with Douglas. That whole nexus of tightly linked passions—to act, be a performing artist; to be successful; to be worthy of Doug, not disappoint him, hold him: that tangled knot had been sliced with brilliant cleanness. She was in love with one Lambros Talouris, rising executive in the shipping business, who attended perhaps two plays and three movies a year, who had never heard of Lee Strasberg and the Actors Studio, who was spiritually most at home on the island of Paxos in the Aegean Sea, and who had thought of her all her young life as someone from the beach in the Hamptons, a tall blond rather athletic girl who was interested in acting, and had done a few things in that line. To him she was

Alexandra Reed of Portals, Water Mill, Southampton, Long Island. That was also who she was to herself. The other, the star, was a construct. Since Doug had been so vital in erecting it, Doug of course was in love with the construct.

She started to sigh as she lay there prone in bed, and then the apparatus, the respirator, the tubes, intervened: you did not, could not, do anything as emotional as emit a sigh when you were hooked into a life-support system: forget sighing. Breathe. Get your discipline reassembled. Not too much nor too little air: breathe.

29

Since I was her cousin, faithful, younger, admiring Nick, Axie had eventually communicated the facts of this episode of the man on the motorcycle to me.

It was August of the summer following her first Paxos visit, and she had become Mrs. Lambros Talouris the previous March. We were sitting on the beach in Water Mill, a beach called Flying Point, where a channel was sometimes bulldozed across the beach so that the ocean could flow into and out of Mecox Bay, our bay, flush it out as you would a bowl. What an odd, remarkable fact of nature eastern Long Island was: a place where nature stood revealed, submitted to manipulation, cooperated. Only rarely did a rogue hurricane howl in from the ocean to wreck and kill.

As we sat on the firm, ivory-colored sand, the beach

here flat and wide under the sun, there were relatively few other people in sight. In these safe surroundings Axie told me about the man in the red dust. "When did you tell Lambros about it?" I asked edgily.

"I never told him," she said. "He heard about it, gossip, and he believed it. And I couldn't deny it, not to him. Besides, I saw that this outrageous thing I'd done was making me interesting to him, for the first time. That's a little outrageous too, isn't it? But that's the way it was."

"And then you told Spyro," I said.

She turned her head to look at me over her shoulder, chin down, a quizzical, somewhat mocking gaze. Then the low, penetrating voice demanded, "Are you mad? You don't think I would tell *Spyro* that, do you! You know him, you know his nature. He is an *idealist,* and he would be *shattered* if he knew that about me. They're so different, the two brothers—half-brothers. Lambros, like most Greeks, can accept anything, he is shock-proof. Spyro is half Greek and half stiff-upper-lip British, kind of old-school charge-of-the-light-brigade. There are certain things *you do not do.* And I'd done one of them, in broad daylight, with a complete stranger. I couldn't tell Spyro *that!* He would have been cut to the quick . . . wherever that is. Where is your quick anyway? Does it ever hurt?"

"Stop changing the subject."

"Very well then: Honesty is *not* the best policy, not always. You don't always unburden yourself on someone you love and who loves you. *Why* should I inflict that on him? It was my reaction to that island, that iconlike island . . . Paxos was like some mysterious statue of a god, very archaic god everybody had forgotten about, nobody knew the meaning of any more . . . but still the faceless great kind of figure survived, and it scared me and sort of

threatened me and so I rushed into the arms of a native of
the place—probably I was just a lusting bitch too. But was
I going to tell *that* to Spyro? Be serious. I *loved* the man.
I wanted to make his life happier. You're crazy, you know!"
and she shoved me rather hard against the shoulders, and,
not expecting this attack, I fell back into the sand and Axie
grabbed my head, giggling fiercely, and ground it into the
sand.

Finally I grabbed her forearms very firmly and forced
her away from me, sitting up. "Let's go swimming," she
cried, springing up. "Look at that surf! Just right. Not too
big, not too small. Not much undertow today too, I see.
Come on." She never wore a bathing cap, but, hair loose,
sprinted across the sand and, dashing through the shallow
water, dived through the first large oncoming wave, I
catching up to her at that point so that we cut through the
wave together and, surfacing in the smooth after-wave,
two rather similarly-shaped heads of the Reed family from
Vermont, we took to the surf of Water Mill.

At one point, when a set of big waves had passed by
and there was a momentary lull, we were standing up to
our shoulders in the sea and Axie fixed me with her eyes.
"You will never repeat what I said to you to a soul. Will
you." I gazed solemnly back at her and said in a serious
tone, "No, I never will. I promise." She looked out to
sea, utterly unconcerned now, completely secure in my
promise. And I never have communicated it to anyone,
until now.

Axie had not been interested in a big wedding. Big
weddings were for her fashionable classmates at Purcell
Academy and members of the Meadow Club and the
Southampton Bathing Establishment. Therefore, they were
not for her.

Nevertheless she was a romantic, and she and Lambros had been married the March following her visit to Paxos at sea on an ocean liner en route to Europe and Paxos. It was all romantic and private and no relative of either bride or groom had been present at the marriage nor on the island. It was for them and only for them.

30

"I was not afraid of him, you see," she explained to me once, a couple of years later, when I commented on the unusual isolation of their wedding, Italian crew members acting as witnesses, the captain giving the wedding breakfast, no one else aboard ship knowing. "I was not wary of him either," she went on, over lunch in the Edwardian Room of the Plaza, looking out from time to time through the huge window at Central Park. "I think most women, and probably most men, too, are basically *afraid* of the person they marry, in love, we hope, but still awfully wary. 'I'm committing myself, my precious self, to *you*!' they wail inwardly. 'How awful!' They're scared. Well," she took a mouthful of steak tartare—raw meat, one of her favorite dishes; Axie was not a shrinking violet—"I wasn't afraid of Lambros, not at all. Mostly, I think, because I knew not him but his *family* so well. I simply felt safe. I *knew* I was safe. The only question was: Was he safe with *me*! That was the question hanging over our marriage."

"Well?"

She looked up at me, scrutinizing my face. "What do you mean, 'Well'?"

"Has he been safe with you?"

She shook her head from side to side, smiling with her eyes at me. "What will I ever do with you?" she then exclaimed. "After all these years, even *you* don't trust me!"

No, I reflected very inwardly, I don't trust you, not a hundred percent. I love you, always have, always will, but trust you entirely, never.

Axie at this time was rehearsing a Broadway musical version of that first hit movie of hers, *The Provincetown Story*. This in itself was unusual; hit plays were almost as a matter of course turned into movies, but this production was taking a successful movie of five years before and turning it into a musical for the legitimate theater. "It's because they couldn't think of anything else to do with me," Axie explained as we walked briskly down Sixth Avenue toward the theater district after lunch. "My last two movies didn't do so well, you see, and nobody's come along with a really good play. So, Doug is putting this vehicle together for me."

Doug was faithful, ever faithful; Axie had virtually jilted him in marrying Lambros, but Doug was faithful.

She inspired that kind of loyalty in those around her. Edna was devoted; I was ever there; wild horses couldn't tear Spyro away. We were all, along with a number of others, quite simply vital elements in her life, and she in ours, and apparently nothing could alter that.

Of course the fundamental trait of Axie's tying us to her was her intense loyalty to us. Saying that she had "jilted" Douglas was unfair; she had never been promised to him, had throughout their affair signaled to him that

that was what it was, an affair, and would not develop into anything more lasting.

We walked west to the large Mark Hellinger Theater, where the musical version of *The Provincetown Story,* retitled *Waves!,* was scheduled to begin previews soon. Axie went to her dressing room and changed out of the Chanel suit she had worn to the Plaza and into black slacks and a white blouse. She pulled her hair back from her face and bound it at the nape of her neck with a rubber band. She had put on virtually heelless dance slippers. There was a big dance number, a kind of jig with sea chanteys, which the choreographer now began to lead her through at one end of the stage, a piano accompanying. He had made a few last-minute changes she had to learn.

At the other end of the big stage Doug was leaning over a card table, discussing the lighting with two men. Today was Sunday, and the theater was otherwise virtually empty.

After he had finished, Doug walked over to me and put an avuncular hand on my shoulder, smiling. He was always pleasant to me, but this was more openly friendly than before. I realized why: we were in his territory, the theater, not in Southampton or anywhere like that; it was possible for him to show me that he liked me better here.

After all, in his eyes I was still a student while he was now a successful man of the theater. I was in fact in everybody's eyes still a student, working toward a PhD in Russian history. I was fascinated by the field but chafing under the status: graduate student. It often seemed that I had always been one and always would be one. Taking in, taking in, and then regurgitating. When would I be allowed to give, express, originate?

How creative it seemed here in the theater on that

Sunday. Doug had written and directed the movie and was now doing the same for this play. Axie was starring. The man working with her now had created the dances, more or less designing them out of thin air, I supposed. A large, owlish fellow who lived on Staten Island had written the music and lyrics. A very busy lady from California had done all the costumes. Someone else designed the sets. All of them around this production were expressing them-selves in one way or another. And I was currently analyzing eighteenth-century peasant revolts in the Ukraine.

"Let's go sit in the orchestra and take it easy," said Douglas. "Axie is just going to have a little run-through with Peter, and there's not much else we can do today. Tomorrow of course this place will be pandemonium again. Ah, the theater, the theater. Why didn't I take up teaching, like you?"

"I like being around the theater," I said as we went over the catwalk across the pit and down some steps to the seats. "There's a creativity about it."

He glanced at me. "That's what takes us all in," he said drily. "Then when we're hooked we find out it's dusty and slavery and usually produces a flop." We settled into front-row seats. "Not that I think this will be," he added hastily. "It's a great vehicle for Axie, and she'll carry us to success. The public loves her as Carrie, they did in the picture, and they will in this."

"You know how to write for her as nobody else does."

He gazed pensively before him, started to comment, then didn't. I could put into his mouth the words he almost uttered: "That's because I love her." He would have said them, her being married or not being married, to anyone else. But I was family, so he refrained. Then he went on: "Axie's not a dancer, but Peter's giving her what she can handle, and with a lot of skillful professionals behind her, the numbers are coming together well. She's not a singer, but if you put the right song in the right range she can do it very effectively. She does some recitative too, and very well. She has a remarkable voice, as we all know, speaking voice. She just has it, always has had it. Never had a singing or a speech lesson in her life. Lots of *acting* lessons and training, of course, from me and other places. So. She's kind of *playing* the role in this, she's giving an interpretation of a musical comedy star doing this musical. Does that clear everything up? No? Well, *she* understands it, and that's all we need now." He squeezed my knee absently. "You will too when you see her on opening night."

After quite a while the choreographer finished with her, and Doug, lithe, sprang out of his seat, clearly forgetting that I existed, and was up on the bare stage with Axie, talking in low tones to her stage center. Bareness was all around them, no sets yet in place, vastness, motes in the air, a bare electric bulb, stuffy air. The theater.

31

Axie and Lambros immediately after their marriage had moved into a big apartment on Gracie Square overlooking the East River. As we were leaving the theater that day, Axie, having simply thrown a mink coat over her rehearsal clothes and left what she'd worn at lunch in her dressing room, seemed very tired. On the street she said to Doug and me, "Come on up to the apartment. Lambros won't be in from the country yet. *Don't* make me rattle around in that mausoleum of an apartment alone."

Axie did not want to be alone. "I would prefer to pick up a bum out of the gutter and take him home to play pinochle than to be alone," was one of her milder explanations. "I *hate* it. I think I am going to die sometimes, when I am too long alone."

"Come on," she persisted, on the sidewalk on Eighth Avenue. We hailed a taxi and started uptown through Central Park.

Sitting between us, she leaned back, her dark blond hair against her collar and the plastic of the seat, and sighed. "New York looks pretty today, doesn't it." We were in November, past the washed clarity of October days, but over the city there now hung a rather portentous grayness which lent a significance to the slight undulations and almost-bare trees of the park, with the slender towers beyond. The city seemed indeed a powerhouse in suspended animation during this breathing-pause of Sunday, a stirring but not a frenzied place today, prams and bicycles and a few horse-drawn carriages and joggers. Even our taxi driver did not seem nervous today.

"I like it here," she went on ruminatively, "when I'm working. Working hard. Otherwise of course I'm a country girl. Thank God Lambros is too." She paused and then giggled a little. "Gosh I must be tired. Lambros really isn't a country *girl* at all. I don't think such a thing as a girlish Greek exists." She sighed again and then seized Doug's hand. "Are you happy today, darling? What do you think?" She did not need to add "about the play": there was nothing else to think about.

"I'm thinking about eighty-five things, and to tell you

the truth—" he gave a rueful laugh—"I don't really know what I think about any of them." He sat silent for a little and then murmured, "It'll be all right." He never humored her, never tried to lift her spirits. They were past that, both knowing that if her spirits were to be lifted, she had to lift them.

I had to put something in: "You did say the show was going to be a hit."

"Oh yes," he said philosophically.

"Do you think so, Nick?" she asked, sitting up to look at me.

"Sure . . . why yes . . . I only heard the composer sing some of the songs in your apartment and—"

"I don't know," she said, settling back. "I'm not optimistic."

And that was true, and always had been true of Axie. She was a practicing pessimist. And that was the last thing that people who knew her by her work, knew her by her "image," by the news stories about her, from television interviews, from all public sources, that was the last thing they expected. She called herself, just among us, a pessimist. I thought there was a certain overstatement in this; she was not a pessimist really, in my opinion. She was simply a rock-bottom realist, with a little extra emphasis on the negative side. That way, she was rarely disappointed.

We reached the apartment. There was a long beige-brown-gray living room with long couches and cube chairs and a collection of glass, with a splendid view of the river and the Triborough Bridge. Next to this there was a small, square, elegant rosewood library, and then the apartment went on into a big dining room and kitchens and large bedrooms. The place could indeed have seemed like a mausoleum to anyone who had to be alone there for too long. It was an exhibitionist kind of domicile, with its large marble-floored entrance hall, and the wide chandeliers, the important paintings. It had necessarily been designed, by Lambros in conjunction with an adviser, for receiving important people. Axie had not taken much interest in it beyond liking its proximity to Carl Shurz Park, and the striking view from the long windows. It was watertight, wasn't it? You could sleep very well in it, couldn't you? There was lots of space for entertaining friends, wasn't there? That was really all she asked.

The three of us were sitting in the rosewood library, reading lamps turned off, the room's angles softened by indirect, subdued lighting. "I have to start thinking about the way I'm lighted," Axie had exclaimed recently, "I'm thirty-one years old this year."

Through the arching entrance to the room I could see the big front door of the apartment, and after a few minutes it opened, and Lambros, in a black tailored overcoat and carrying a gleaming briefcase, came in. He tossed coat, briefcase and hat on a settee and came on into the library, crossing to Axie, who, as she invariably did, had preempted one end of the only couch in the room. Lambros kissed her, nodded in a relaxed way to us, and collapsed into a low-slung, overstuffed armchair.

"Tired, darling?" Axie inquired archly. "That's what good little wives of overworked businessmen ask at the end of the day, isn't it?"

He cocked an eye at her. "You would be too if you'd cut short your weekend in the country, taken a plane in at five o'clock in the morning, broken into this place to change into these clothes to meet Dad and some damn Armenians on the *Pacificus* at the yacht basin, and been there negotiating ever since."

Axie frowned compassionately at him, and then swiftly uncoiled from the couch. "You really *have* had an awful day. And I was feeling sorry for myself because of *my* Sunday! You need a drink and you need it now, and I'm going to get it, of course, and what do you want?"

He was gazing up a little quizzically, amused, at her. "Scotch. A splash of soda."

"Goodness," she murmured, moving out of the room, "you have had a hard day. Almost straight whiskey. Not like you. Nick, find out what Douglas wants and fix yours."

After that, we settled around this intimate room. In his dove-gray French suit and Charvet necktie and razor haircut, Lambros was groomed differently from Axie in her slacks and Doug in his sneakers. "I guess you must have been working at the theater today," he said.

"Just a couple of little things," put in Douglas. "Once the show is set and then after we open Axie will only be working a couple of hours a day. I know we've been kind of monopolizing her lately."

Lambros turned to look at her. "You're enjoying it," he asked smilingly, privately.

Axie cast her eyes upward. "I don't know that 'enjoying it' are the words I'd choose. More like 'enduring it' because it'll be so nice when it stops. The rehearsals, I mean, the changes. Once it's set, yes, I think I'll enjoy it, even love doing it, for a while. If, God willing, we should have a long run, then, well, then I think it'll begin to bore me."

"That's when you'll show you're a professional," said Doug intently.

"Yes," she concurred, "yes."

"And you *are,* you know," he said across to her, privately.

"Yes," she agreed.

"When am I going to see it?" inquired Lambros easily.

"*Not* before opening night!" Axie semi-shouted. "*Never.* It must be perfect before—well, as close as we can get it. You will *not* see us fumbling around."

"Well, not exactly fumbling," muttered Douglas.

"How do you like it so far?" asked Lambros, turning to me.

"I only heard what you heard, the composer running through the score at the piano here. And then today, well all I saw was Axie doing some dance steps."

There was a short silence and then Lambros asked, "Is there anybody in the kitchen?"

"I didn't know what time you were coming in," replied Axie, "so I let them both have the evening off."

"Good," said Lambros decisively. "Then I'll take everybody to Pavillon, for a treat," and he beamed at us. Then we all realized what Douglas was wearing; Axie could change out of her slacks and blouse.

"Listen," Doug began quickly, "I've got to be getting back downtown because—"

Axie cut in decisively: "You will *not* be getting back downtown, and we will *not* be going to Pavillon! You understand, darling?" she said, turning to Lambros. "Listen. I can cook. Nick!" and here the sense of command she possessed was fully employed: I virtually jumped to my feet, "you and I will go into the kitchen and leave them here to talk about . . . talk about . . ." she began to half-smile half-wickedly . . . "the weather or something, and we'll bring out supper here on trays, and that's it! *D'accord?*"

"Axie, I really—" Doug began.

"Shut up."

"Fine," said Lambros agreeably.

32

Just a little more than two years later, I attended with Lambros Talouris the final performance of that smash hit musical, *Waves!*

This was by now the sixth time I had seen it, and as I watched Axie doing the big dance number in her saloon with the fishermen, who had just rescued Carlo from a knife fight on the dock, I thought she got through it with just as much verve, just as much freshness, as on opening night. She very definitely was the professional Doug had said she was. "Oh that goddam *number!*" she had moaned to me. "And to think they almost dropped it from the show before we opened! If only they had! Now I have to do it eight times a week. From now to eternity, I guess."

And *Waves!* might have approximated such a run, except that the star finally could not face that number or the show in general after eight hundred and seventy-six repetitions, and so it was closing. Replace Alexandra Reed as Carrie? That was impossible. The show would not have lasted through to Saturday night, and the producers, one of whom was Douglas Shore, knew it.

It was during this run that I came to whatever understanding of the theater I will ever have. The relentless toil of rehearsals, with, in the cases of *Waves!,* many revisions and new scenes and revised scenes, added dances and subtracted songs, miscues, and crises and slips, had at last been ground through by everyone concerned, the play had opened and it was a big hit, and I presumed it would be smooth sailing from then on.

But there was one proviso: they had to perform it every night except Sundays, and twice on Wednesdays and Saturdays. I had not apprehended what this really meant until I witnessed, almost accompanied, the run of this musical.

It had had its triumphant opening early in December, with the big party afterward, and then I had gone back to my graduate work at Harvard. I finished class work that June, bummed a trip to Europe on a Talouris tanker, visited Paxos, where I had their house to myself for a while, and then went on for a prolonged sojourn in Russia, mostly in Leningrad.

Leningrad was a little like the other side of the moon. Or else, it was traveling in a time machine back to Peter the Great and the Romanovs and their palaces and their great plush theaters and their wide straight boulevards. The chill canals of the city, the strange, lowering sky; the reeking restaurants with their oblivious waiters eventually serving dubious food but lots of booze; the secretiveness of this wide-open-looking city; these and a thousand other impressions and experiences began to transform me, as living in remote places will, into someone else, a modified version of myself, not a Russianized one at all but into an American with a new angle of vision, perceiving the United States somewhat differently, with a new appreciation of its strengths, and a sighting of some of its limitations. I glimpsed new strengths in me too, and also, to be sure, in me too, previously unsuspected limitations.

This entire trip lasted a year.

Then, when I did return to America and happened to drop in on a performance of *Waves!*, I found Axie and all the others in the cast still saying the same lines and singing the same songs.

I couldn't believe it. I knew about long runs theoretically, but now I was actually seeing actors carrying a play through such a run, one of these actors was Axie, and now I began to sense what being in the theater must be like.

It was clearly like nothing else on earth. It was a kind of cloister. The alternative to the numbing repetition Axie and everybody else on that stage were enduring consisted of being unemployed, sitting at home by the telephone. It made me understand that, close as she and I were, she belonged to a sisterhood and brotherhood utterly apart from me and everyone else not in the theater; it was as though they were all in the army together, at war somewhere, and when they at last came home they knew they could never tell us what it had been like, that, try as we might, we could never understand.

If this was true of me, it was even more true of Lambros.

He and I sat side by side, eighth row center, through the final performance. Axie was shining with true star quality that night: the whole Talouris family was there, Edna was sitting out front, Axie's parents had come, and her special friend Madge from the days at Purcell, and while I had never seen her give anything less than a good performance, tonight she added that slight extra twist to her lines, gave just a hairsbreadth more completeness to her moves, concentrated on meanings in song lyrics one more time, and, at the end, brought down the house.

There were two parties, one for everyone in the cast and their guests and many other people in one of the new discotheques, and, after we had been through that one and Axie had spent enough time there so that no one could think that she had slighted this party in any way, there was a second party in the apartment on Gracie Square. There were her parents, that is, my cousin Harold Reed and his wife Hannah; Edna Purvis; all the Talourises; the school friends; Douglas Shore with his current lady, a Danish sculptress named Ingrid; and my parents and me.

The capacious, softly lighted rooms seemed to glow with contentment, not the excitement of beginning but the satiation of the end, of completion. Axie was wearing a long, dark blue velvet gown which laid quiet emphasis on her femininity, as she glided from group to group, seeing that they all had champagne or cognac or mineral water, and reminding them about the buffet in the dining room. In the background, unobtrusively, the sound system in the apartment was playing a special arrangement—all instrumental, no voices—of the music from *Waves!* The party floated on this undercurrent of beat and melody, and while I would have thought the people thoroughly sick of this score by now, they instead seemed buoyed by it as a background to carry them through the evening, one final time.

Through the long, wide windows the few lights of late-night Queens across the water gleamed with the placidity of anywhere. It was a New York nighttime episode here in this apartment: *Waves!* was exclusively this city's show. It had not gone on a tryout tour out of town but simply offered previews here in Manhattan, and there was to be no national tour now or ever. The show had opened, succeeded, enjoyed a long run, and was now closing, in Manhattan. There was to be no movie either. "Lightning doesn't strike twice in the same place," Axie's agent had pointed out: one hit movie had already been made of this material.

Axie in blue was a feminine creature tonight, hugging people, squeezing, kissing, a relaxed and graceful actress in her element, one she had created and now could savor, passively, attending to her guests, as self-forgetful as she ever got.

She barely had time to speak to me, and I understood it; we were always close, never lost touch; other people, dear to her and not nearly as accessible as I, were here tonight to be woven once more into her life.

In front of the square fireplace, of Paxian marble, I talked with Axie's father. Six-feet-two, broad of shoulder and authoritative of voice, he was a formidable figure in New York banking circles and in this room tonight and wherever he went. As we stood there that night I was more certain than ever of what I had long surmised: that Axie's character was really based on him. Turn Cousin Harold into a woman, which seemed unthinkable, and you would produce Alexandra, and, unthinkable or not, it had been done. Feminine Axie, all woman, was somehow derived from this stalwart man.

Standing beside him was perhaps the reason: Mrs. Reed, Hannah, Axie's mother. Hannah was fragile and birdlike and pale and passive and faint-voiced and How, I sometimes asked myself, had Axie come out of her? Axie as a little tot, an only child, had looked around her, looked from mother to father and at the age of three, four, six, sometime, had been irresistibly pulled into focusing herself on daddy, not on mother, focusing on him as the main person to love, but not just to love, also to resemble, to emulate, to, in a certain sense, become.

Bemused, sniffing my Courvoisier in front of the fire as Cousin Harold told me that *Waves!* had paid back its investors three hundred percent or something like that, I concluded that this was the source of her uniqueness: a very feminine heterosexual girl had based her self-image on a strong, commanding man, her father, whom she loved more than anyone on earth. Axie was hardly able to speak to him tonight either, and, even more than with me, that didn't matter.

Spyro was there with his wife of four years, Janie Peters from Connecticut, a young woman for whom field hockey had been invented, Axie said. She had already produced two children. For her, quite simply, all questions in life were black and white, and if, perchance, Spyro said that one was the other, then she would accept that and live by it ever after.

Lambros Talouris was sitting with my parents on the long couch with its back to the view. He had not met them before. As a classics professor my father had a thorough knowledge of Greek and of Greece, at least classical Greece, and since Lambros knew the modern one thoroughly, they were absorbed in conversation. Mother, who loved, raised, showed and bred German shepherds, including Axie's Bruno, and who had made her human contribution, she apparently felt, by bringing me and my brother into the world, now gazed with a pleasant, abstract expression into the middle distance, as the two men leaned toward each other, conversing back and forth in Greek and English. Later Lambros told me that talking to my father in Greek was like talking in English to some gentleman who spoke Elizabethan.

Then the big front door flew open, and this party, which had been a family and school-friends kind of gathering, went into transition. In swept the other two producers and their wives and the composer-lyricist and his friend and several members of the cast and the lady who had done the costumes and Axie's agent and her publicist and some regulars from Sardi's and some other theater people, friends and acquaintances and friends of theirs whom Axie in her euphoria had invited at some point or other during this last *Waves!* evening. The background music seemed to get louder and the party faster; it was approaching three in the morning and this party was now going to move into full swing.

Axie drifted through the crowded rooms and I could see that, even more than the last triumphant curtain calls for *Waves!,* this was the peak moment of the memorable night for her, this was what she had striven for, not the crash of applause and cheers coming across the footlights from faceless strangers but a room full of specific people whom she loved and who knew and loved her, this was what getting through the damn big dance number eight hundred and seventy-six times had been all about, just this, a room full of happy celebrating family and friends who were happy for her, and loved her.

Lambros was, as always, a perfect gentleman, as my mother would later observe, but at some point after the party had moved into this much higher gear he had quietly withdrawn to his own suite of rooms and gone to sleep, or at least gone to lie down, and hear, faintly, through the apartment's sturdy interior walls, the long diminuendo of Axie's triumph.

EIGHT

33

On her seventh day in intensive care, Axie's injuries and therapy entered the phase of horror.

Until now, there had been a kind of cottony blur to all she went through, a lapsing into fantasy and half-recollection; utter fatigue too had cushioned her, and the protective mantle known as shock.

Now, however, she was emerging from these partial shieldings to confront the edge of death continually, over and over, twenty times a day, and night, maybe thirty, maybe more.

It began, quietly and insidiously enough, with a gradual accretion of phlegm in her lung. This accretion would begin to clog the bottom of her breathing tube, and the only means of escaping death by choking was an ordeal called Suction, which had to be repeated each time she felt the fatal accumulation approaching the critical point.

As she felt herself begin to choke, Axie would press urgently on the button summoning the nurse. Rather casually, one of the nurses would enter, sometimes promptly, sometimes not, and insert a thin tube down the larger tube in her throat and at a certain critical point this inserted tube would induce, suddenly and violently, a paroxysm of vomitous coughing, spewing up some phlegm and shooting razory pains from her broken ribs throughout her right side.

And this had to be repeated, and repeated, and repeated, until day became night and all time merged into this deadly and protracted ordeal.

I know what I could do, she thought with a kind of winter calmness at one three o'clock in the morning. The next time that menacing accumulation begins to mount I could do nothing, I could just not push the button; it would surely all be over in a matter of a minute or two, I can feel that. The blockage will be complete; I will not be able to breathe.

I will just die, quietly, here, alone. I will die of breathlessness. Yes, maybe that is it.

Why in God's name not? I have nothing to live for. I turned away my husband, my self-contained Lambros, who loved me in his own detached, worldly, bemused way, who had never met anybody like me and it could have gone on, if I had not let my career come first. No children, because of my damned "tubes"? He could have borne that heavy disappointment, if I had devoted myself to him. I caused the failure of our marriage.

What did I do really with Douglas except to use him?
I drained him dry of every last thing he knew about acting
and about me specifically as an actress. I kept luring him
into creating vehicles for me, which might have been a
reasonable demand to make upon him while I was his
lover, but after, even after, when I marched off and got
married I *still* insisted, insidiously insisted on his working
for me. For example, *Waves!* He never wanted to rework
the material of *The Provincetown Story* into a blaring Broadway musical, but I inveigled him into it. And he in his
loyalty and enduring love for me dropped the challenging
projects he had before him in his growing success, turned
back, and hacked out a competent vehicle for me.

You really are a selfish bitch, she murmured to herself.

And as these winter thoughts would turn and turn in
her head, gradually the deadly fluids would accumulate in
her lung and creep slowly and then less slowly to the point
where air, and soon after it life, would be choked off.

I have no husband, and I have no child.

Her cubicle in intensive care now seemed grayish white,
all of it, the sheets, the walls, tables, window, floors, the
occasional faces that appeared, her thoughts: all were grayish white. Color had been drained from the universe, and
even the photograph of the agora on Paxos appeared to
have lost the bright island hues and faded into the gener-
alized noncolor of this cubicle.

In the middle of, Axie thought, the second day at this
ultimate ordeal, this Suction, Edna crept in, not her shoul-
ders-back Edna but a deteriorating being, a little hunched,
a shade cringing, beaten down. Axie saw that not only she
but Edna was having to pass through this, and a pang, a
sense of something, responsibility, momentarily struck her.

The nurses had finally been prevailed upon to untie

Axie's hands after fervent written promises that she would never no *never* touch the respirator. But she had realized now that by literally not lifting a finger she could end her life. No need to knock the respirator dramatically away and so reveal her suicidal intentions: she just had to do nothing, and nature, baleful nature, would take its course, the horrible phlegm accumulate, the tube become blocked, and breathless she would pass out of all this and into whatever there was.

Baleful nature: and she, in her white house with its deep porches beside her charming cove with the three swans, and the bay beyond and the sandbar beyond that and then the ocean, she had floated with such confidence and almost voluptuous ease on the nature which there surrounded her, so sure of herself; dear beautiful safe Mother Nature had smiled at her, beamed down upon her with all the beneficent rays of the Long Island sun. She had been so sure and so safe and so blind.

Well she was no longer blind; in lying here dragging herself back from asphyxiation over and over there was one bleak compensation: now she saw. She saw, amid the grayish whiteness of her cubicle, the kind of woman she had been, and she also now saw what kind of a force nature was. Nature had two faces, the one she had always before beheld, and this other one, flashing menace and threats and suffering and death.

Edna crept into the cubicle, and Axie was able to raise her left hand, which Edna fervently grasped. Then she moved to a little stand against the wall and put something on it: a plant. It was an odd little growth in a terra cotta bowl, just long green strands growing upward and then curving rather gracefully down, a humble little plant, but growing. "Something green," muttered Edna, "this room needed something green. I know they don't allow flowers in here—so many flowers have been sent, the house is overflowing with them because the hospital won't take them—but if not flowers, maybe they'll let you keep this." She turned and looked down almost piteously upon Axie. "Is there anything I can do, can I do anything? You know, smuggle anything else in? I don't care about regulations."

Axie was seeing a new side to Edna: Edna the Law-breaker. No one had been more conformist until now.

Axie shook her head slowly, fondly, and, calling once again on her powers as an actress, stopped the tears from coming.

And then the accumulation began to gather in her lung, the menace began to accumulate—the opportunity, the escape?—and she did not want Edna to witness this. This could destroy Edna, the Suction, the paroxysm. Pushing the button, she simultaneously motioned with her hand, and Edna, instantly understanding, quickly vanished. Then the nurse came in with the little tube and casually, slowly, lowered it bit by bit down the larger tube in Axie's throat until the electrifying instant when her being was spasmodically wrenched to the core.

And now alone, with the little green tendrils of the potted plant offering the only color in her universe, Axie, with a strange heated feeling gathering in her body, turned her face toward the act of suicide.

I am in a position now, she reflected tensely, when if I decide to do it I can do it. I could not before, because it would have been known for what it was. If I had accumulated many pills and taken them all. If I had knocked away the respirator. Whatever. ACTRESS SUICIDE IN HOSPITAL. That would have been page one on the *Daily News*. Axie would never do that to other people, shake their own hold on life by taking hers. Well-known, admired people who commit suicide shake everybody's grasp of life, sometimes profoundly. She would never do that in a thousand years to a world which by and large had been good to her, never dream of doing that to all those young women who saw her stride through a movie and wanted to be like her, to those young men who watched her move and heard her voice and sensed in themselves a desire for her. Never. Let them know she had taken her own life? Never in the world.

But this way: the horrid accumulation of phlegm simply gathered a little too fast for her, the nurse a little too lackadaisical in getting to her room, the emergency sliding into crisis faster than anticipated and then—*snuff*, off with her life, gone.

She could do it; she knew she could.

She leaned her head rather painfully back further on her pillow, tried to draw a little extra air from that inexorable and judicious machine which rhythmically pumped life into her by the numbers: If I had had a child . . .

34

Dr. Wainer had an office on East Sixty-second Street in New York, and he had before him on his desk the papers showing the results of all the tests Axie had taken at his direction. He was long, pale and thin, and his voice was as expressionless as everything else about him.

"Well, Mrs. Talouris," he began with deliberation, "it's clear, the situation."

He had been slow of speech and he had formulated his thoughts very systematically, step by step, and it had been several minutes before she could grasp the simple fact that she had an inner obstruction which prevented her becoming pregnant.

Waves! had been closed for six months, and Axie had not accepted the two or three film offers which had arrived. She had accepted no work at all; she and Lambros were now going to start a family.

Greek men were fathers who had children, especially sons, and Greek women produced them as a matter of course. Lambros was in most respects more at home in the Dorchester in London than he was anywhere in Greece, except when it came to fundamentals such as this. Then he was just a Greek like any other.

After what seemed to her a kind of hiatus there in Dr. Wainer's office, a period when she sat and he just gazed at her saying nothing, Axie rose and thanked Dr. Wainer and left.

At home that evening she settled with Lambros after dinner into the snug rosewood elegance of the small library in their apartment, holding a little cup of Italian coffee. Lambros, she was relieved to see, had helped himself to cognac.

Finally she spoke, her voice controlled. "I got the results from Dr. Wainer today."

He looked across at her and she read in his eyes comprehension and sudden disappointment: because she had waited throughout the day until this relaxed, easeful moment to speak of it, her news was going to be negative. Axie watched Lambros grasp that, she watched comprehension and deep disappointment and then finally resignation come into his face. She had never loved him more, never cared for his happiness more.

"Yes," she said quietly, "it's what you think. There's some obstruction."

After a silence, he said: "Could you have an operation? Would that stand any chance?"

She just shook her head, smiling grimly.

He settled back and his hands fell down on his thighs. "Well, that's it then."

"Lambros."

"Hm? Yes?"

"I don't want to adopt any children, I can't explain why, I maybe am too much of an egomaniac."

He chortled briefly. "Egomaniac," he echoed disparagingly. "I don't want somebody else's kids around here either, to tell you the truth."

"You don't have to stay married to me." She threw the line like a lance, like a javelin flung into space.

He looked quizzically over at her. "What are you saying?" he then demanded.

"I'm saying," she went on quietly, "that you don't have to stay married to me. That's what I'm saying."

"Axie. Sweetheart. I love you. You know that. You do, don't you? Listen. We won't talk any more about it."

And they had never mentioned the subject again until, three years later, with her career once again in high gear and his comprehensive trips keeping them increasingly apart, Axie and Lambros had listened to Norma as she showed them, separately and together, that their marriage had reached impasse and should, before their love for one another turned into something else, end.

35

At dusk on Axie's eighth day in intensive care, Spyro Talouris materialized beside her bed. She was horrified to see him. At any moment the terrible fluid might begin accumulating in her lung. Then she would either choke to death before his eyes or go through the repulsive ritual of Suction in front of him. How to get him quickly out of the room?

"Axie," he began huskily, "your color's better. You're beginning to look like yourself again. As soon as they can take those damn tubes out of your mouth . . . and nose . . ." he seemed to have to enumerate them, ". . . and ribs . . . and arms . . . then you . . . you'll look like yourself again. Everybody sends a lot of love. What do you need? Here's the pad and the pencil. Write."

She scrawled in her block letters: TO BE LEFT ALONE EXHAUSTED FORGIVE LOVE. Spyro stood above her, tentative, dubious. The phlegm was building, her air thinning, her panic rising. Convulsively, driven, she pushed the button. This time the nurse was prompt.

"What are you doing here?" she snapped at Spyro, brushed him aside, pointed the thin tube in her hand into Axie's wider breathing tube, probed slowly further, then further and abruptly Axie's body spasmed, and phlegm and blood shot up from her damaged lung into the little tube, which the nurse slowly withdrew.

Head back, mouth agape, Axie was flung back on her pillow.

"You must leave," ordered the nurse.

"One second," said Spyro starkly, rigid. He approached the bed. He took Axie's hand, squeezed it. "You've always been the bravest woman I know," he said in a low voice. Then he turned and was gone.

Have I been, have I been! Axie demanded inwardly, almost scornfully. Is that what you're counting on, that I'm brave enough?

36

I had waited in my car in front of the hospital while Spyro made this surreptitious visit.

When he came down, he flung open the door, threw himself on the seat beside me, hunched forward and growled, "Let's get the hell out of here. Fast." He slammed the door shut.

I glanced over at him as I moved the car away. "What's the matter?"

"She's being tortured to death in there," he snarled. "She's dying. She's being pulled apart."

"What're you talking about! Yesterday her signs were better."

There was a silence from Spyro and then he muttered, "You didn't see her. I did."

"What'd you see?"

His hands clenched together. After a moment he let drop one expressionless word: "Death."

"I don't know what you're talking about," I said.

He sat staring in front of him, and then he muttered almost wheedlingly, as though hoping I would argue him out of it, "I don't see how anyone can live through that."

At Portals, Pauline Marsh was slumped at one end of the long white couch in the living room. We paused at the entrance of the room and Spyro just looked at her, beheld her. Pauline glanced at us, fidgeted a little, looked down again at her magazine. "How is she?" she finally murmured uncertainly.

"Look—ah—Pauline, Miss Marsh," began Spyro in a, to me, surprisingly reasonable voice, a very exasperated but still in-control voice, "why don't you leave now? Go home. You must have a home somewhere. Why don't you go there?"

Pauline had filed several on-the-whole inoffensive stories about Axie's ordeal, stories which had been played less and less prominently in her newspaper. There was after all no further news in them. I suspected she was lingering here because she thought there was a very long magazine article in this material potentially, a series, even a book, especially should Axie die.

"I'm staying for any further news. There will be some, don't you think so, Nick?"

I took a long breath. "No, I don't think so. I don't think your paper does really, either. The story's over, the newspaper story. She's not a star any more. It was just that photo you took. It was so sensational, and there wasn't much news that weekend. That's why it got such a play all over the world. But there isn't any news left here. There really isn't. Actually, as a reporter, I think you're wasting your time."

A light went on behind Pauline Marsh's eyes. I had, at last, flicked the right switch. This reporter was lingering where there was nothing any longer left to report.

After an interval that can barely be described as decent, Pauline Marsh went upstairs and began to pack, and within thirty minutes she was gone.

That afternoon I heard a car pull in and stop in the driveway, and in a few moments Norma and Lambros came into the living room. Norma wore a filmy pastel dress and a big hat; Lambros wore espadrilles, white pants and a blue shirt. The colors of Greece, I thought automatically.

Then Spyro came swiftly into the room. "I've just been on the phone with Dad in New York. Axie's having spasms or something like that in the hospital. She's being wracked. She can't live through this," he added reasonably, as though trying to convince us of some utterly unreasonable proposition. "But Dad says his doctors check continually with her doctors and everything is being done right. It's something about her lung. She has to go through these attacks or whatever they are to clear out her lung." His voice sank to a mutter. "She's not going to live through this. Nobody could. If you'd seen her."

"I think we now have to pray," murmured Norma.

"Why didn't you take care of her?" Spyro demanded bluntly of Lambros. "The doctors say the whole fall at the party was probably really due to stress, nerves, tension.

You should have been there with her these past years. You shouldn't have gotten divorced. Didn't you know what you had? What your responsibility was? To take care of her, for Christ's sake. Her parents are *dead*," he said with self-evident reasonableness. "*Somebody* had to look after her. Why didn't you?"

Lambros grimaced, said nothing, sat down at the far end of the couch.

"Why did you marry her in the first place, then?" Spyro persisted, struggling to keep reasonableness in his tone. "I'm the one who should have married her," he added, throwing the words away.

Lambros's head came up and he stared at him. "Was that what you wanted? You never showed it. At least I never saw it. And, to get right to the point, I don't think Axie ever saw it either."

Spyro's face fell for an instant into a strange expression. I think I interpreted it right: this was the great void and lack in his life: he had never made his move for Axie.

It was his terrible void, and to cover it over he characteristically attacked. "You even let the people on Paxos get away with that damn lie about her before you got married, making it with some guy in the dirt! You never really protected her. You should have started right then. Why didn't you?"

Lambros gazed evenly across at him. "Because the story was true," he said quietly.

The strange expression again sprang for an instant onto Spyro's face, more starkly this time. Another horror to be faced. "You're nuts . . ." he growled, "lying . . . crazy . . ." He got up. "I'm not going to stay here and listen to this right in her house. You won't even defend her now. You never did deserve her. I've had it with you, Lambros. Don't call me and I won't call you."

For a rather queenly woman, Norma could move surprisingly swiftly when she wanted. She caught Spyro's arm before he could get out of the room, and slowly turned him back into it. "Come and sit down, sit back down, and don't speak that way to your brother. I'm not going to allow this thing to destroy the family. For one thing, Axie would hate being responsible for that. There. Sit down there. Now I'll sit back down here. Listen to me, dear, just listen. Axie didn't hurt anybody that day, long ago now, when she apparently . . . gave . . . in to that man on Paxos. There must have been a lot of reasons. She's brilliant. She was exhausted. You left her alone. She hates being left alone. It's her curse, her fear. We all have one. It's hers. The only thing that's hurt now is your, well, your dream of her. It's always been so unrealistic, the way you picture Axie. All the way back to your school days together. She was like a Viking goddess to you. And I . . . after all, I can remember how she looked. You had this dream of her then . . ."

Spyro had been almost imperceptibly closing in on himself as she spoke, and Norma now got up and walked quietly across to stand over him, looking tranquilly down at his head. "You're so awful, Spyro," she then said with a chuckle. "Always have been so awful. So mean. But you're really . . . a kind of angel at the core, aren't you. My embittered angel."

Spyro still sat there, not moving, huddled, protective of himself, and of that dream.

37

The light was fading in her cubicle, so she guessed it must be early evening now, the grimmest time of day. Spyro had been gone for many hours, but he had seen her agony and the look on his face had told her the rest: he had been shocked to the core; he did not think she could live through this.

But Axie knew better; the doctors had told her this horrific way of draining her damaged lung was a step toward recovery, it would end in a matter of days and her recovery would proceed. It simply looked, sounded, and felt like death; it was, in fact, a step back toward life.

But who wanted that?—as the light faded to shroud-like grayness among her sheets—sheets on the bed, sheet-like partitions surrounding her; she was sheeted and swathed about with gray linen, wrapped in a pall already, in the failing grayish last of sunlight.

All through these last days, Axie had felt intermittently a kind of void forming around her.

If only she could speak to someone! No one had been more verbal, voluble, self-expressive in words than she; they had been one of her lifelines. And now mute, fed and pumped up by tubes, drained too by them, she had lost this line to life. She was wordless. She could not tell them. The void widened, as though by erosion, day by day and hour by hour around her. She was unable to talk her way

out of it, and so it insidiously increased in size, grew as
the hateful phlegm at the bottom of her lung—bottom of
her life—grew, very slowly and horribly and threateningly
until she felt that she could not stand it another moment,
this creeping into her and all around her of menace and
threats and, above all, below all, around all, emptiness.

There seemed to be no support for her anywhere.
What was there, what did she have? Make a litany, a list:
no father, no mother, no brothers or sisters, no husband,
no children, no career.

Terrifying in its sterility and lack of support, this vision of her place, her nonplace, in life was nudging her
on: Don't press the button next time, don't; it will all be
over in a minute or two. Otherwise ahead of you there is
nothing but struggle, to regain your health and strength
if you ever can at age fifty; struggle with the dregs of a
career, and the burnt-out ends of relationships; and decay,
the decay of aging, in your body, your mind; struggle
with the remnants of your beauty.

She dozed. The episodes of Suction came at such in-
tervals that prolonged sleep was impossible. Now she dozed,
and did she see it in her semidream or did she in reality
see it, the funny tendrils of the odd little plant Edna had
brought? Skinny, greenish, curving little tendrils, springing up from a bulb at the center of the little bowl and
curving down to the tabletop. Living. It was a quasi-cactus
sort of a plant, needing a little water, not much, but some.
It had not been watered.

She pressed the button; the nurse came. In pantomime
Axie told her what to do: water that plant, and bring it
back. And she continued to doze.

There was a light breeze blowing outside her window,

and passing through leaves, ruffling them gently: leaves.
Green.

The breeze was playfully and gently passing across
the leaves and there was a responding gentle sound of their
ruffling and sinking back. And she could hear the ocean—
or could she?—and it echoed and reechoed and continued,
and would continue, and would continue.

And the ocean and the leaves and the funny little plant
and the crickets—and she Axie was alive still too and this
life was precious and unknowable and the gift sublime and
could she give it up, will it to end, could she could she,
No she could not however miserable. No, not with the
ocean and the crickets and the plant and the unknowable
future. It was a gift, it had been presented to her and she
must guard it just on principle because you never knew
and selfishness, yes, even her selfishness had its limits and
she must cling to this life for life's sake and forget your
own "remnant of beauty" and all else and just take life as
something unknowable, like that raw reddish cliff of Paxos,
the unknown statement just take it and go along with it
and don't argue and forget yourself, you're not so special
and you have your roses to prune and Bruno to walk and
people to teach to act, so shut up and go to sleep. And
now the phlegm began to gather one more time and swiftly
too this time, and she fumbled around, rather convulsively
now among the gray shroudlike sheets because she could
not locate it at first and there, there was the button and
she pressed it urgently.

38

Then one bright day, two mornings later, after the birds had finished their first screechings and the intensive care unit began to hum with its purposeful tasks—transfusing a bleeding patient, wheeling out a dead one—Dr. LaBrianca entered her cubicle and approached her bed in a somewhat different way, a purposeful way. A nurse was with him, and they did little things here and there and then Dr. LaBrianca came over her, his face above hers, and his hand came toward her face, and he grabbed all the tubing and before she knew whether anything hurt or not he snatched all the tubes away, out of her, all of them. Freed!

"Is that better?" he inquired a little humorously.

Better! Her throat was now her own, no longer a piece of plastic.

She drew a breath unaided, she asked for air and her lungs drew it in. She could breathe, naturally.

But could she speak? It seemed a very long time, an eternity, since she had used her voice. Was it still there, and what did it sound like? Would she, the sudden risible question posed itself, ever sing again?

"Yes, doctor, I feel better," she said slowly, in a kind of gruff tone, ragged, but recognizably her own. "I feel . . . *much* better! Oh so very very much *better*!"

"The therapist will be here soon, about your lung.

And then. We've got to get you out of that bed! On your feet!"

And these sentences of his inaugurated the new phase of her recovery, the next mountain range to be scaled. The therapist, a young woman—"Aren't you pretty!" remarked Axie—brought an odd plastic kind of toy, three vertical tubes with little Ping-Pong-like balls in them and a rubber tube with a mouthpiece attached. By inhaling desperately deeply on this Axie tried to create vacuum in all three tubes and force the little balls to the top. Four laborious days later she succeeded in getting all three of them there, once, for a split second.

They made her sit up on the side of the bed. Strange! Dizzying and puzzling. She nevertheless sat there for five minutes, and her robe happened to be parted and her thighs revealed. Whose were they! Shrunken, seemingly muscle-less, they could not be Axie's famous shapely, svelte legs. But they were. "They'll come back," remarked Dr. LaBrianca. "Work."

"Work" this time meant being placed in the center of a large contraption on four wheels, with supports under her shoulders, and in this she made her way rolling up and down the corridor, her weak legs, her damaged right side, gradually beginning to function. Then on into a walker, something she had seen people eighty years old and older use if they were especially feeble, something that now she, Alexandra Reed, was going to use, if she had the strength for it, the balance, the courage.

And she saw herself as others must see her, the patients and staff of the hospital, dragging her thin body in a long white gown slowly along the corridor. A broken, aging woman, surely? Discarded by life now, for her sins, her pride.

39

August lapsed into September, and clogged Montauk Highway now had only light traffic. Scallops came into season, and September stillness settled calmly over the East End.

The day came when Axie was released from the hospital. She was wearing a long white robe as Spyro and I pushed her, seated in a wheelchair, out the entrance and then helped her into the rear seat of a long limousine. The car then rolled away through the fresh September morning. "So green," murmured Axie, more or less to herself, staring out the car window.

As we turned off Montauk Highway onto Cobb Road the force of the ocean began to be felt, we could not yet hear it or see it, but there was a hovering vastness which could be felt. Axie settled back against the seat and stretched her spare body, as though something tight were now flowing out of it.

When the car came to a stop in the circle of gravel in front of the East Porch, Axie told us to put the walker, not the wheelchair, in front of the car door, and she maneuvered herself into position with it and, haltingly, advanced toward the porch.

"Just let me sit here on the porch, darlings, just let me sit and look, sit and stare. Edna, be a dear and just put that chair facing the cove and the bay, and *Bruno,* how wonderful, he doesn't jump up on me even *today*—he hasn't forgotten his training, not even today—" for Bruno was going into a mad dance around her legs, leaping up and dropping down but always avoiding touching her, as he had been trained, making burbling noises in his frenzy of joy but not forgetting that he had been trained not—ever—to jump up on Axie or anybody else.

She settled into the straight-backed wooden chair and just gazed at the view, her view, across the slope of lawn down to the little cove and the still sheet of bay water beyond, and the distant strip of sandbar.

Then Edna persuaded her to go up to her room, and Spyro and I carried her there.

One by one, or in groups of two or three, everyone who formed the structure of Axie's life came in the next weeks to see her at Portals: Lambros came with his wife Elena and their elder son, after which Lambros departed on his next trip to Japan; Spyro and Janie came, bringing their two youngest children, then left for the house they had rented in Washington, as Spyro took on a long-term assignment with the State Department; Douglas called on her alone, and the following week flew to Nepal for a prolonged shooting schedule on his new movie; not long after their joint visit to Axie, Norma and Stamos departed to spend the autumn on Paxos. "You will come to us there," said Norma in farewell.

And then there was me, and the Saturday morning came for my postponed departure to resume teaching at the University of Vermont.

Axie was prone on the couch on the East Porch, morning cup of coffee balanced on her stomach. Her head was resting on her left hand. A cane, replacing the walker, leaned nearby. I kissed her. She drew one of her long, deep, dramatic sighs. "So now you too say good-bye to me."

"Yes." I must have been looking at her in a certain kind of way.

"If you start feeling *sorry* for me, darling, I'm going to kill you."

"Oh Axie, I could never feel sorry for *you*," I protested, and as I said these words I wondered whether they were now true or not.

"I will be here," she said, "I will be alone, with my devoted Edna and my devoted Bruno, but, you know, in a sense really alone. The one thing I feared more than anything else in life. I know you will come and see me, I know you will come often. So will everybody. You all know where to find me. I will be here. You know me, Nick. Loyal. I will be here."

"*And you will travel!*" I put in encouragingly.

"Yes. Oh yes. Back to Paxos, one of these days. I don't suppose I'm a scarlet woman there, any more."

I drove away and she lay there alone. Axie then heard something; a faint deep pounding far off: the surf. But it couldn't be; not even the sea at its highest could be heard at this distance. This echo of the sea's pounding was in her imagination, her memory.

How salubrious it sounded, illusory or not.

It's only September, she reflected; I've often gone into the sea this late, later, much later in the season.

Before this season is ended, before the chill closes in on us, I'm going to go down to the beach—no walking cane, I soon won't need that—and I'm going to go into the sea, just a little way, this time, just stand there as the last rush of the waves comes up to me.